The Boxcar Children
Surprise Island
The Yellow House Mystery
Mystery Ranch
Mike's Mystery
Blue Bay Mystery
The Woodshed Mystery
The Lighthouse Mystery
Mountain Top Mystery
Schoolhouse Mystery
Caboose Mystery
Houseboat Mystery
Snowbound Mystery
Tree House Mystery
Bicycle Mystery
Mystery in the Sand
Mystery Behind the Wall
Bus Station Mystery
Benny Uncovers a Mystery
The Haunted Cabin Mystery
The Deserted Library Mystery
The Animal Shelter Mystery
The Old Motel Mystery
The Mystery of the Hidden Painting
The Amusement Park Mystery
The Mystery of the Mixed-Up Zoo
The Camp-Out Mystery
The Mystery Girl
The Mystery Cruise
The Disappearing Friend Mystery
The Mystery of the Singing Ghost
Mystery in the Snow
The Pizza Mystery
The Mystery Horse
The Mystery at the Dog Show
The Castle Mystery
The Mystery of the Lost Village
The Mystery on the Ice
The Mystery of the Purple Pool
The Ghost Ship Mystery

The Mystery in Washington, DC
The Canoe Trip Mystery
The Mystery of the Hidden Beach
The Mystery of the Missing Cat
The Mystery at Snowflake Inn
The Mystery on Stage
The Dinosaur Mystery
The Mystery of the Stolen Music
The Mystery at the Ball Park
The Chocolate Sundae Mystery
The Mystery of the Hot Air Balloon
The Mystery Bookstore
The Pilgrim Village Mystery
The Mystery of the Stolen Boxcar
The Mystery in the Cave
The Mystery on the Train
The Mystery at the Fair
The Mystery of the Lost Mine
The Guide Dog Mystery
The Hurricane Mystery
The Pet Shop Mystery
The Mystery of the Secret Message
The Firehouse Mystery
The Mystery in San Francisco
The Niagara Falls Mystery
The Mystery at the Alamo
The Outer Space Mystery
The Soccer Mystery
The Mystery in the Old Attic
The Growling Bear Mystery
The Mystery of the Lake Monster
The Mystery at Peacock Hall
The Windy City Mystery
The Black Pearl Mystery
The Cereal Box Mystery
The Panther Mystery
The Mystery of the Queen's Jewels
The Stolen Sword Mystery
The Basketball Mystery

The Movie Star Mystery
The Mystery of the Pirate's Map
The Ghost Town Mystery
The Mystery of the Black Raven
The Mystery in the Mall
The Mystery in New York
The Gymnastics Mystery
The Poison Frog Mystery
The Mystery of the Empty Safe
The Home Run Mystery
The Great Bicycle Race Mystery
The Mystery of the Wild Ponies
The Mystery in the Computer
   Game
The Mystery at the Crooked
   House
The Hockey Mystery
The Mystery of the Midnight Dog
The Mystery of the Screech Owl
The Summer Camp Mystery
The Copycat Mystery
The Haunted Clock Tower
   Mystery
The Mystery of the Tiger's Eye
The Disappearing Staircase
   Mystery
The Mystery on Blizzard
   Mountain
The Mystery of the Spider's Clue
The Candy Factory Mystery
The Mystery of the Mummy's
   Curse
The Mystery of the Star Ruby
The Stuffed Bear Mystery
The Mystery of Alligator Swamp
The Mystery at Skeleton Point
The Tattletale Mystery
The Comic Book Mystery
The Great Shark Mystery
The Ice Cream Mystery
The Midnight Mystery

The Mystery in the Fortune
   Cookie
The Black Widow Spider Mystery
The Radio Mystery
The Mystery of the Runaway
   Ghost
The Finders Keepers Mystery
The Mystery of the Haunted
   Boxcar
The Clue in the Corn Maze
The Ghost of the Chattering
   Bones
The Sword of the Silver Knight
The Game Store Mystery
The Mystery of the Orphan Train
The Vanishing Passenger
The Giant Yo-Yo Mystery
The Creature in Ogopogo Lake
The Rock 'n' Roll Mystery
The Secret of the Mask
The Seattle Puzzle
The Ghost in the First Row
The Box That Watch Found
A Horse Named Dragon
The Great Detective Race
The Ghost at the Drive-In Movie
The Mystery of The Traveling
   Tomatoes
The Spy Game
The Dog-Gone Mystery
The Vampire Mystery

# THE BOXCAR CHILDREN DOG LOVERS' SPECIAL

## MYSTERY AT THE DOG SHOW
## THE GUIDE DOG MYSTERY
## THE MYSTERY OF THE MIDNIGHT DOG

created by

### GERTRUDE CHANDLER WARNER

ALBERT WHITMAN & Company
Chicago, Illinois

The Boxcar Children Dog Lovers' Special
created by Gertrude Chandler Warner

ISBN 978-0-8075-0883-1

10 9 8 7 6 5 4 3 2 LB 14 13 12 11 10 09

Cover art by Robert Papp.

For information about Albert Whitman & Company,
visit our web site at www.albertwhitman.com.

# THE DOG LOVERS' SPECIAL

# THE MYSTERY AT THE DOG SHOW

### created by
## GERTRUDE CHANDLER WARNER

*Illustrated by Charles Tang*

ALBERT WHITMAN & Company
Morton Grove, Illinois

Printed in the U.S.A.

# Contents

CHAPTER                       PAGE

1. A Dog Show in Greenfield      1
2. Watch Makes a Friend      12
3. The Polka-Dotted Couple      26
4. Dog Walking      36
5. The Mysterious Man      46
6. A Bad Haircut      58
7. A Surprise for Sunny      72
8. An Unexpected Visitor      81
9. Sunny Disappears      94
10. And the Winner Is . . .      111

CHAPTER 1

# A Dog Show in Greenfield

"Faster!" shouted six-year-old Benny Alden. "I'll race you to the bottom of the hill!" He leaned over and started pedaling his bicycle as fast as his short legs could go down the long hill at the end of Wildwood Road.

"Hey," said Jessie, Benny's older sister, who was twelve. "You have a head start." She pedaled after Benny. A moment later Benny's older brother, fourteen-year-old Henry, and his other sister, Violet, who was ten, were racing after Benny, too.

"It's a tie, it's a tie!" shouted Jessie as the four Alden children coasted to a stop at the bottom of the hill.

"No, it's not," said Benny.

"What do you mean, Benny?" asked Violet. "We all got to the bottom of the hill at exactly the same time."

Benny shook his head and pointed. "You forgot Watch. He got here before all of us!"

The four Alden children all looked at the happy, panting dog. He had come to live with them when they first became orphans and were living in an old abandoned boxcar in the woods. They'd been on their own, trying to take care of themselves. When a dog had limped into their lives with a thorn in his paw, it had seemed only right to take care of him, too. So Jessie had taken the thorn out and Benny had named the brave little dog Watch. He had been a good friend and watchdog, too, ever since.

Now the Boxcar Children no longer had to live in the boxcar in the woods. They hadn't known it then, but they had a grandfather who had been searching and searching for them. He'd found them at last and brought them all to live in his big, wonderful old house in Greenfield. And he had even had their boxcar moved to the backyard behind the house, so they could visit it whenever they wanted.

"Arf!" said Watch.

"Look at Watch." Henry laughed. "He knows he won!"

Watch ran around them in a big circle, wagging his tail so hard it looked like he was about to fall over.

"Okay, Watch," said Jessie, laughing too. She threw up her hands. "I give up. You're right, Benny. Watch is the winner!"

"Good boy, Watch," said Benny. "Hooray for you!"

"Arra-arrf!" answered Watch, making them all laugh harder.

At last Henry took a deep breath and managed to stop laughing. "Hey, we'd better be getting back home! It's almost dinnertime."

The four Alden children and Watch turned toward home. They'd been at the

Greenfield Park all afternoon. It had been a wonderful day.

They were almost home when Jessie suddenly put her brakes on and coasted to a stop.

The others stopped, too.

"What is it, Jessie?" asked Violet.

"Look. There's Dr. Scott's office. Isn't it time for Watch to have his annual shots for rabies and distemper and everything?"

"You're right," said Henry. "Let's go in and make an appointment right now."

They walked their bikes over to the side of the veterinarian's office building and parked them. But when they got to the front door, Benny said, "I'm not going in."

"Oh, Benny," said Violet. "Why not? You like Dr. Scott."

It was true. Benny did like Dr. Scott. They all did, ever since they'd helped out at the Greenfield Animal Shelter, where Dr. Scott sometimes worked.

"Yes, *I* like Dr. Scott," agreed Benny. "But *Watch* doesn't like to go to the veterinarian's office. He doesn't like to get shots! So I'll stay out here with Watch."

Henry smiled. "You're right Benny," he said. "I don't think anybody likes to get shots, even though they are for your own good. You can wait here with Watch and we'll be right back."

Henry, Jessie, and Violet went inside. Benny sat down on the steps next to Watch and put his arm around the dog.

"Don't worry," said Benny. "I'll go in with you when you have to get your shots."

Watch wagged his tail and put his paw on Benny's arm.

Inside the veterinarian's office, the receptionist looked at the three Alden children over the top of his glasses and smiled. "Hello," he said. "What can I do for you?"

"We'd like to make an appointment with Dr. Scott for our dog, Watch," explained Jessie.

"I'm sorry. Dr. Scott is away on vacation. Another veterinarian is handling her patients if there's an emergency," the receptionist told them.

"No, it isn't an emergency," said Henry. "Could we make an appointment now to see

Dr. Scott when she gets back? Our dog Watch needs his annual shots."

"Certainly," said the receptionist. He ran his finger down the page of the appointment book. "I have an appointment right after lunch the first day Dr. Scott's back in the office."

"Great," said Henry.

"Please make it in the name of Watch Alden," Violet said.

With a smile, the receptionist wrote *Watch Alden* down in the appointment book, then wrote the time and date on a card and gave it to the Aldens.

After thanking the receptionist, Henry, Jessie, and Violet went outside to join Benny and Watch. They rode quickly home to join Grandfather Alden for dinner.

As always, Mrs. McGregor, the Aldens' housekeeper, had made a wonderful dinner. And as always, Benny had seconds of everything and still had plenty of room for dessert.

"Ummm," said Benny, starting to eat the warm apple pie with ice cream that Mrs. McGregor had made for them.

Henry shook his head. "You have a *big* appetite, Benny."

"I'm still a growing boy," said Benny. "That's what Grandfather says, isn't it, Grandfather?"

Grandfather Alden chuckled. "It certainly is," he told his youngest grandchild. Then he reached in his pocket and pulled out a letter. "Before I start my dessert, I want to share some good news with you all."

"What is it, Grandfather?" asked Violet.

"This is a letter from my old friend Mrs. Annabel Teague. She and her daughter will be in town next week for the first annual Greenfield Dog Show at the Greenfield Center."

"Neat," said Jessie. Then she smiled. "I can solve the mystery of why she's coming, too!"

Grandfather's eyes twinkled. He knew his grandchildren loved mysteries and that they were very good at solving them, too. "What is the answer, Jessie?" he asked.

"She's going to be *in* the dog show," guessed Jessie.

His eyes still twinkling, Grandfather said, "Well, not exactly. *She's* not going to be in the dog show — but her golden retriever, Sunny, is!"

"Oh, Grandfather," laughed Jessie, and the others joined in, enjoying his little joke.

Then Violet asked, "What are the Teagues like, Grandfather?"

"Well, Mrs. Teague is a kind, generous person. I haven't seen her daughter, Caryn, since she was a little girl, but I remember she was a smart, active child. She's sixteen now, and it's no surprise to me that she's the one who will actually be showing Sunny in the dog show."

"How exciting," exclaimed Jessie.

"Yes it is," said Grandfather. "Caryn has had plenty of practice, it seems. Sunny has won lots and lots of prizes with Caryn showing her."

"Oh, may we go to the dog show?" asked Benny. "Please Grandfather? And see Sunny?"

"Of course, Benny. We'll all go." Grandfather paused and looked solemnly around

the table. "But . . . how would you like for
the Teagues and Sunny to stay with us while
they're here for the show?"

"That would be great!" exclaimed Benny.

"Yes," said Jessie.

Henry and Violet agreed, too.

"Good," said Grandfather. "I'll get in
touch with Annabel right away to make
arrangements."

"Maybe we can help Caryn get Sunny
ready for the show. We can help give Sunny
a bath and brush her and take her for walks,"
said Violet.

"I wonder what else you have to do to get
ready for a dog show," said Jessie thoughtfully. "I bet we'll learn a lot. I can hardly
wait!"

"Can we enter Watch in the show?" asked
Benny. "He could win lots and lots of prizes,
too!"

Grandfather hid a smile. "I don't think so,
Benny. You have to be a certain kind of dog."

"Watch is very brave and smart," said
Benny.

"But he's not a particular breed of dog,"

said Henry. "I think only special breeds of dogs can be in a dog show."

"Yes," said Grandfather. "For this dog show, your dog must be registered with the American Kennel Club. The dog's mother and father have to be registered, too."

"Oh," said Benny. He looked at Watch, who was sitting by the dining room door. "Well, that's okay, Watch. You don't mind, do you?"

Watch tilted his head. "Arrf," he said, and they all laughed.

# CHAPTER 2

# *Watch Makes a Friend*

"Benny! Benny, where are you?" Jessie was trying to find her brother.

She looked into Violet's room. "Have you seen Benny?"

"No." Violet shook her head. "Did you ask Henry?"

"Not yet." Jessie started down the hall to Henry's room just as he came out. "Henry, have you see Benny? It's almost time for the Teagues and Sunny to get here."

"I'm ready," said Henry. "But I haven't seen Benny. Have you looked in his room?"

Jessie nodded. "Yes, but he's not there."

"Maybe he's downstairs with Mrs. Mc-Gregor. It sure smells like something great is cooking," Henry said.

"That's a good idea. Thanks." Jessie went downstairs to the kitchen.

But Benny wasn't there.

"Mmm, it smells good, Mrs. McGregor," Jessie said, taking a deep breath.

Mrs. McGregor smiled, "That it does. There's nothing that smells as good as fresh-baked bread. Or that tastes as good, either."

"I can hardly wait," said Jessie. "It smells so good, I was sure Benny would be in here."

"No, he's not. But I have an idea if you check out back by your boxcar, you might find him," suggested Mrs. McGregor.

"Thank you," Jessie said, and hurried out the back door.

Sure enough, Benny was in front of the boxcar. He had filled an old tin washtub full of soapy water, and he and Watch were covered in water and suds.

"Benny! What are you doing?" Jessie called.

"Giving Watch a bath so when he meets Sunny, he'll be nice and clean," gasped Benny, trying to hold on to the squirming dog. Watch thought having a bath was great fun. He was splashing in the water and wriggling all around.

"Oops," said Benny, waving his arms and trying to keep his balance as Watch bumped into his legs. He tripped and fell into the washtub with Watch.

Jessie started to laugh as soap and water flew everywhere. Benny stuck his head out of the water and wiped his face. He grinned. "I guess I'll be clean, too," he said.

"I guess you will. Here, let me help you," said Jessie. She gave Benny a hand out of the washtub. Then the two of them caught Watch and soaped him all over and rinsed him gently with the hose.

"I remembered to bring a towel," said Benny proudly. He went over to the boxcar and picked up the towel he had left on the tree stump that was the boxcar's front step. Together Benny and Jessie dried off Watch.

"Watch is beautiful," declared Benny.

"He does look good," agreed Jessie. "Now, we must hurry and get ready. The Teagues and Sunny will be here any minute!"

Jessie and Benny rushed back to the house to change into clean, dry clothes. As Benny went up the back stairs into the kitchen, he looked over his shoulder.

"Don't you want to come in, Watch?" he asked.

Watch stayed where he was at the foot of the back steps.

"Okay, you can stay outside," said Benny. "But be good, now. And don't get dirty!"

The front doorbell rang just as Benny and Jessie finished getting ready. They raced down the stairs as Grandfather Alden opened the front door. Henry and Violet were there already.

In the doorway was a small woman with blue eyes and red-gold hair twisted back into a soft bun. She was wearing khaki slacks, a plaid shirt, and a blue cardigan sweater. She stepped briskly over the threshold and gave their grandfather a big hug. "James Henry

Alden," she said. "It has been a long, long time."

"Much too long, Annabel Teague," agreed Grandfather Alden, smiling.

In a moment, two more figures appeared in the doorway.

"This is my daughter, Caryn," said Mrs. Teague. "And of course, Sunny."

A tall graceful girl, who looked about sixteen, followed Mrs. Teague into the house. She had hair the same red-gold color as her mother's, but her eyes were brown instead of blue, and she wore her hair pulled back in a single braid. She was wearing khaki pants, too, and a red pullover sweater.

Caryn was holding a red leash in one hand. At the end of the leash was a large golden-red dog with silky, slightly wavy fur.

"Sit, Sunny," said the girl in a quiet, pleasant voice. The dog sat down and looked around with a friendly expression on her face.

"Wow," said Violet.

The girl held out her hand. "How do you do, Mr. Alden?"

"I'm glad to see you again, Caryn," he answered, shaking her hand. "You won't remember this, but the last time I saw you, you were just a little girl. You've grown up, I see."

"I hope so," said Caryn, laughing a little.

Grandfather Alden bent over. "And this is Sunny," he said. He stroked the top of the dog's head. "She's a beauty."

Both Caryn and Mrs. Teague looked pleased. "Champion Gold Doubloon's Morning Sun," Mrs. Teague said. "That's her registered name. Of course, we call her Sunny."

"Well, let me introduce my family," said Grandfather. "These are my grandchildren, Henry, Jessie, Violet, and Benny."

Everyone shook hands. Then Benny held his hand out to Sunny.

"Benny, I don't think . . ." Grandfather began.

But Caryn smiled. "Shake, Sunny," she said.

Sunny held up her paw and shook hands with Benny.

"You're a smart dog!" cried Benny.

"Maybe you can teach Watch how to shake hands, Sunny. Watch is our dog. His full name is Watch Alden, but we call him Watch. He's smart, too."

Benny went to the front door and opened it. "Watch," he called. "Here, Watch!"

But Watch didn't come.

"He'll be here soon," said Benny confidently, closing the door.

Grandfather said, "Meanwhile, why don't we take you to your rooms and let you settle in. Then come down for something to eat and drink. You must be hungry after your trip."

"I have a special traveling kennel for Sunny," said Caryn. "May I set that up in my room? It's big enough for her to move around in and to keep her food and water in."

"Of course," said Grandfather. "Although she's so well-behaved, you don't need to keep her in there unless you want to."

It didn't take long for the Teagues to settle in. Soon they were all sitting around the kitchen table, eating fresh baked bread with butter and honey, and drinking milk or tea. Caryn had brought Sunny back down with her. When they'd reached the kitchen, she'd pointed to the corner by the door and said, "Down Sunny." Sunny had laid down. "Good girl. Stay," said Caryn. And Sunny had stayed there ever since.

"Does she do that at the shows?" asked Henry, looking admiringly at Caryn.

Caryn shook her head. "You're talking about obedience trials," she told Henry. "They're not part of this show. This show is about how a dog looks and acts. The judges look to see if it walks correctly and has the right color coat and the right kind of ears for its breed."

Violet looked puzzled. So did Jessie and Henry. Benny was twisting around in his chair looking for Watch, so he wasn't listening as intently as everyone else.

"At a show," Caryn explained, "each dog is walked around the ring while the judge watches. Then the judge looks at each dog more closely. The dog that's closest to perfect for its breed is the winner. So on the first day, Sunny will compete just against other golden retrievers."

"Oh," said Violet, looking less puzzled. "I think I see."

Caryn smiled. "And there's more. All the breeds of dogs are divided into seven different groups — Sporting Dogs, Non-sporting Dogs, Working Dogs, Herding Dogs, Terriers, Hounds, and Toys. Golden retrievers are in the Sporting Dog group. If Sunny is the best golden retriever, on the second day she'll compete against other kinds of sporting dogs, like Labrador retrievers and Irish setters."

"What if she's picked as the best in the Sporting Dog group?" Henry asked.

"Then on the last night she'll compete against the winners of the other six groups to see who is the best dog in the whole show."

"Wow," said Jessie. "The winner must be a terrific dog!"

"I can hardly wait to see all the dogs," said Violet.

"Yes," said Henry. "We're going to come watch the show and cheer for Sunny."

Caryn smiled at their enthusiasm. "Why don't you come to the show tomorrow?" she asked. "It doesn't really start until the day after, but people will be arriving and getting their dogs used to the place. It will be fun. There'll be a lot to see and do."

"That would be great!" said Henry.

Just then there was a scratching at the kitchen door.

"Watch!" exclaimed Benny happily. He rushed to the door and opened it.

Watch bounded in and stopped. His tail went up, and he started wagging it stiffly. The fur on the ruff of his neck stood up. As plainly as if he'd said it in English, he was asking, "Who is this strange dog in *my* kitchen?"

Sunny raised her head.

"Okay, Sunny," said Caryn. "Be good, now."

Sunny stood up. She and Watch touched noses. Gradually the fur on Watch's neck went down. Suddenly he put his two front legs flat on the floor, while sticking his hind-

quarters and tail up in the air. He wagged his tail furiously.

"He's saying, 'Let's play!' " Caryn laughed.

Everyone watched, smiling, as Sunny did the same thing as Watch.

"Would you like to go outside and play, Sunny?" asked Caryn.

"May we take them out, Grandfather?" asked Violet.

Grandfather laughed. "If it's okay with Mrs. Teague."

"Just be careful that Sunny stays in good shape for the show," said Mrs. Teague.

"Don't worry," Caryn said. "I'll keep an eye on Sunny. I'm sure nothing will happen to her."

"We'll show you our boxcar, too," said Henry. During their snack, they'd told the Teagues a little about their adventures in the old boxcar.

"I'd like that," said Caryn.

Everyone except Grandfather and Mrs. Teague went outside into the late afternoon sun. Watch and Sunny began to run in happy circles, barking and dancing around each other.

Henry led the way to the boxcar with Caryn walking beside him. Benny ran ahead and Jessie and Violet followed everyone.

Benny climbed up into the boxcar. "Look," he said, standing in the door. "This is my pink cup. I found it." The cracked pink cup was Benny's favorite possession. He had found it when they were all living in the old abandoned boxcar, and he still used it sometimes.

"It's a very nice cup," Caryn told Benny. She climbed into the boxcar after Benny and let the Aldens show her their former home, telling how Grandfather Alden had moved the boxcar to the backyard as a surprise, after they had come to live with him. Many of the things — the blue tablecloth, the kettle they'd cooked with, the old teapot and pitcher they'd found — were still inside.

"So this is the boxcar," Caryn said admiringly. "How lucky you were to find it! And brave to be on your own like that, too."

"It was fun," said Benny.

Henry smiled at his younger brother. "It *was* fun," he agreed. "But it was hard work, too. I'm glad we live with Grandfather Alden now."

"It's a wonderful boxcar," said Caryn. She and Henry sat down on the front stump and watched as the others romped and played with the two dogs until it was time for dinner.

# CHAPTER 3

# The Polka-Dotted Couple

The Greenfield Center, where the dog show was being held, was a big new building at the edge of town. As the Aldens approached it the next day, they could see cars and trucks and vans arriving, and people hurrying in and out. The sign out front read WELCOME TO THE FIRST ANNUAL GREENFIELD DOG SHOW.

"We've never been here before," said Henry.

"It's *big*," said Violet. "And there are so many people!"

"And dogs," said Benny.

They threaded their way among all the people and dogs and finally reached the back door.

"Look," said Violet, pointing. A sign by the door said REGISTRATION THIS WAY.

A moment later, Henry, who was the tallest, spotted Caryn. "There she is!" he said. He waved and Caryn waved back. She headed toward them, with Sunny walking sedately beside her.

"Hi Sunny!" said Benny happily. Sunny's tail waved gently to and fro.

"Sunny sure is calm around all these people," said Violet. Violet was shy, and being around a lot of people made her nervous.

Caryn smiled. "She's used to it. I've got her all signed in, but I'd like to walk around a little to get my bearings. Why don't you join me?"

"Okay," agreed Henry.

Together they all walked out to the main arena. It was bigger than a basketball court, with rows and rows of seats all around it. But velvet ropes had been strung across it, dividing it into sections.

"Each section is called a ring," Caryn explained. "That means that several different breeds of dogs will be shown at the same time in different rings of the arena. There will be a judge assigned to each ring."

"How do you know when it's your turn? And what ring to go in?" asked Jessie.

"The rings have numbers above them, see?" Caryn gestured. "And the time and ring number is listed in the program for the dog-show owners and handlers and the audience, and for the judges, too."

"It's a lot of work!" exclaimed Benny.

"That's true, Benny. But it's a lot of fun as well," Caryn said. She led them out of the arena.

Suddenly, a man and woman pushed past them, walking a beautiful white dog with black spots. The couple seemed to be dressed to match their dog — the man had on a black-and-white polka-dotted tie and the woman had on a black-and-white spotted dress.

The woman's face was red. "*Why* do we have to keep showing Zonker?" she demanded, grabbing the man's sleeve. "Tell me that! He's a champion now. Why not let him retire and have a little fun?"

"Because Zonker *likes* being a show dog," the man said angrily. "That's what he's bred and trained to do."

"*You* like it. That doesn't mean *Zonker* likes it!" the woman shouted angrily. "I'm tired of this whole dog-show business. For once I'd like to spend a few quiet weeks at home, instead of traveling around trying to win blue ribbons!"

"And *you'd* do anything to get what you want, wouldn't you!" the man shouted back, his own face growing red. "I think you'd actually sabotage a champion dalmation like Zonker — "

Just then, the two people seemed to realize

that others could hear their quarrel. They glanced over at Caryn and the Aldens. Then the woman hissed, "Shhh!" Without another word, the polka-dotted couple hurried out of sight with their dog.

"Maybe it's not so much fun for some people," said Benny.

Caryn sighed. "Maybe not, Benny."

They kept walking past a double door with a sign above it that said BENCHING AREA.

"What is a benching area?" asked Jessie.

"Come on, I'll show you," said Caryn. They pushed through the doors and saw long, wide, low benches. The benches were divided into sections and above each section was a sign.

"The signs are the names of the breeds of dogs," explained Caryn. "During the show, on the day your dog is being shown, you have to keep him or her in a special kennel in the section with other dogs of the same breed. Except when you're in the show ring, or exercising your dog, of course."

"Why?" asked Henry.

"Well, it's a good way for all the people showing dogs to get to know each other better, I guess. And visitors to the show can come and see the dogs up close, and ask questions. If you're interested in a particular breed of dog, like a golden retriever, it's a good way to find out more about it."

"There's the sign for the golden retrievers," said Violet.

"Oh, good. Now Sunny and I will know just where to go. Thank you, Violet," said Caryn.

"Oh no, oh no!" A small, round woman with big brown eyes was standing at a benching area nearby, wringing her hands.

Caryn looked up. "Mrs. DeCicco, what's wrong?"

"It's Ruth Chin," said Mrs. DeCicco. "You know, my assistant. She's usually so reliable. But she hasn't shown up yet. She was supposed to meet me here."

"I'm sure she'll be here at any moment," said Caryn soothingly. "Mrs. DeCicco, I'd like you to meet some friends of mine." Caryn introduced the Aldens to Mrs. DeCicco.

"What kind of dogs do you show?" asked Jessie.

"Beagles," said Mrs. DeCicco.

"Her beagles are famous," said Caryn.

Mrs. DeCicco smiled a little, but she was still obviously very worried.

Violet said, "Um, Mrs. DeCicco?"

"Yes, dear, what is it?" asked Mrs. De-Cicco, looking nervously around.

"Maybe we could help," said Violet.

Abruptly, Mrs. DeCicco looked back at Violet. "What?"

"Yes," said Henry. He put his hand on Violet's shoulder. "What do you need done? We could help until your assistant gets here."

"What a nice thought, dear, but . . . well
. . . well, maybe you could, at that!" She
studied the children thoughtfully for a
moment, then repeated, "Maybe you
could."

"They're very good with Sunny," Caryn
put in.

Mrs. DeCicco nodded. "Very well, then.
I'm staying at the Lamplighter Inn, just
down the road, where most of the show people are staying. If you could come this afternoon and help me exercise my dogs, I would
appreciate it."

"We'd be glad to," said Jessie.

"Lovely, lovely. Then I'll just leave
a message for Ruth at the information desk,
in case she shows up, and I'll meet you
at the inn this afternoon at four
o'clock."

"At four o'clock," repeated Henry carefully.

"Wow," said Benny. "We have a job at the
dog show."

Caryn smiled at Benny. "You sure do. I

think you'll enjoy it. Meanwhile, I think it's time for lunch for all of us."

"I like lunch," said Benny.

"Me, too, Benny," laughed Caryn. "Me, too."

CHAPTER 4

# *Dog Walking*

The Lamplighter Inn seemed to be just as full of people and dogs and hustle and bustle as the Greenfield Center had been.

"How will we find Mrs. DeCicco?" asked Benny, staring.

"We'll ask at the desk," said Henry.

He led the way to the inn's front desk and asked for Mrs. DeCicco's room. Soon the Aldens were on their way to the north side of the inn.

"Here's her room," said Jessie. She knocked crisply on the door.

A few moments later, Mrs. DeCicco answered it. She looked just as flustered as before.

"Oh, good, I'm so glad you came. Ruth is *still* missing. It's not at all like her . . ." Mrs. DeCicco stepped back and motioned for the Aldens to come inside.

Along one side of the room were the dogs, in three large wire cages with flat metal bottoms. Each cage had a different blanket in it, along with dog toys and bowls for food and water. A small plaque above the door of each cage had the dog's name and the name *DeCicco Kennels*.

Mrs. DeCicco handed Violet, Henry, and Jessie each a leash, and began opening the cages. She lifted the first beagle out. "This is Sally. Good girl," she crooned as Sally wriggled and began to lick her face. Handing Sally to Henry, she reached for the next beagle. "Here's Gloria. She's Sally's mother." Gloria and Sally looked exactly alike. Jessie took Gloria and clipped the leash to the dog's collar as Henry had done with Sally.

"And this," said Mrs. DeCicco, opening

the last cage, "is Joe." She handed Joe to Violet.

"What about me?" asked Benny,

"You can carry their dog biscuits," said Mrs. DeCicco. "If they behave on their walk, you may give them each a dog biscuit at the end of it."

"Oh, good," said Benny. He took the three dog biscuits and put them carefully in his shirt pocket.

"Give them a brisk half-hour walk," instructed Mrs. DeCicco. "Don't let them dawdle too much." She had to raise her voice, for the beagles had begun to bay and leap up in excitement, and then to pull the children toward the door of the hotel room.

"See you in half an hour!" called Mrs. DeCicco as the Aldens and the beagles hurried out.

The Alden children didn't have to worry about getting the beagles to walk briskly. They trotted along the street in front of the hotel, heads down and ears flying, sniffing everything. People smiled and nodded as they passed, recognizing Mrs. DeCicco's prizewinners. One woman said, "Ah, the DeCicco beagles. Are you helping Mrs. DeCicco?"

"Yes we are," Henry said.

"It's too bad she didn't have a beagle for you to walk, too," the woman said, turning to Benny. She motioned to the little dog she was walking. "Would you like to walk Britty for a little while?"

"That would be great!" Benny said, looking down at the woman's long, skinny dog. "He looks like a hot dog!"

"He's a dachshund," the woman told him. "I'll wait for you here."

Benny took the leash and the children continued their walk. As they were passing the Greenfield Center, Benny exclaimed "Uh-oh!" and backed up into Jessie.

"What is it, Benny?" Jessie asked.

Benny pointed, his eyes round. A very big black-and-white spotted dog with a square head and pointed ears was being led on a leash toward them.

"Wow," breathed Violet. "That's a *huge* dog."

"Excuse me," said Henry. "What kind of dog is that?"

The tall, thin woman holding the dog's leash smiled down at them. "He's a Great Dane. We call him Berries. Because of his spots, you see?"

Berries lowered his head toward Benny and wagged his tail.

"Is he friendly?" Benny asked.

"Very. Great Danes are a very friendly breed," the woman said.

"I don't know . . ." Benny said, backing away nervously.

"How about if your brother holds his leash, and you can pat Berries," the woman offered.

Handing Sally's leash to Jessie, Henry took Berries's leash, feeling a bit nervous himself. But Berries stayed perfectly calm. Benny reached out and patted Berries's head. Berries lowered his head even more and his tail wagged harder.

"He likes that," the woman said. "Well, I think Berries and I had better be on our

way." Henry returned Berries's leash to her. "Come, Berries," she said.

After they had left, Benny turned to his sisters and brother. "He looked like he would be big and mean," said Benny.

"That just goes to show you can't judge by appearances," Henry said.

"Yes, but you should never pet strange dogs without asking their owners first," Jessie told Benny.

They had now gone all the way around the block, and they saw Britty's owner waiting for them.

"Thank you for letting me walk her," Benny said, giving her the leash.

"Thank *you*," the woman replied.

As they were heading back to the hotel, the Aldens passed lots of other people and dogs.

There were two full-coated collies being walked by a stately man with long, flowing golden hair, and a bulldog being walked by a thickset old man with a mashed-in nose.

"You know, some people look just like their dogs," whispered Violet.

"It's true," said Jessie. "Oh look! Excuse me, what kind of dog is that?"

A short, stout woman with very short, very white hair stopped and smiled at them, while her dog pulled on his leash and grinned a doggy grin. "She's an English bull terrier," said the woman. "Her name is Shug."

They all looked at Shug, who also had very short white hair and was very solidly built. "She looks like a nice dog," said Jessie politely.

"Oh, she is when she wants to be," said the woman cheerfully as Shug pulled her in the opposite direction.

Just then a large, shaggy dog bounded around from behind and stopped in front of them. It was clear from his excited wiggling that he wanted to play. He didn't have a tail, but his whole back end was wagging.

"A sheepdog!" cried Violet.

"An Old English sheepdog, actually," said a voice behind them. A man in a rumpled gray suit, with shaggy gray hair, came up to them.

"He's beautiful," said Violet.

"Thank you," said the man. "He's a champion — Champion Burger Plum Pudding."

"What a funny name," said Benny.

The man raised an eyebrow. "Burger is the name of my kennel where he was born and bred. Plum is from his father's name — Plum Best, you know — and Pudding is from his mother's name, Proof of the Pudding."

"Oh," said Benny. "Hello, Burger Plum Pudding." He began to pat the dog's head.

"I call him 'Plum' for short," said the man, smiling.

"Like Sunny!" said Benny.

"Sunny?" The man abruptly stopped smiling and his eyes narrowed. *"Sunny?"*

"That's the dog who's staying with us. She has a longer name, but the Teagues call her Sunny for short." Henry explained.

"The Teagues," repeated the man. "Well, well, well."

"Do you know the Teagues?" asked Jessie eagerly.

The man stared at them, then turned abruptly without answering. "Come, Plum," he ordered, and stalked away.

Plum hesitated. He liked having Benny pat his head.

"Now," ordered the man sharply.

Plum reluctantly obeyed.

"I wonder what that was all about," said Jessie, frowning as she watched the man march away with Plum trailing along behind him.

"I don't think he liked us," said Benny.

"He seemed to like us fine at first," said Henry, puzzled. "Until we mentioned Sunny. Oh, well, our half hour with these guys is almost up. We'd better get back. We don't want Mrs. DeCicco to worry."

"Do you think Sunny knows Plum?" asked Violet.

"We can ask tonight," said Jessie.

"I think that would be a very good idea!" agreed Henry.

"Is it a mystery?" asked Benny.

"Maybe it is, Benny," said Henry. "Maybe it is."

CHAPTER 5

# The Mysterious Man

That night after dinner, as the Alden children sat on the wide front porch with their grandfather and the Teagues, Jessie said, "Mrs. Teague, do you know someone who has a dog named Plum?"

"Plum?" repeated Mrs. Teague. "Well, yes, I do. That's the name of a rather famous Old English sheepdog that is often at the same dog shows we attend."

"Yes. From Burger Kennels," said Caryn. "He's a lovely dog, friendly and gentle. A beautiful sheepdog."

"Why do you ask, Jessie?" Mrs. Teague inquired.

"We met Plum today while we were walking Mrs. DeCicco's beagles," explained Jessie.

Benny blurted out, "I liked Plum a lot. But I didn't like his owner."

"Oh, you must mean Lawrence Burger!" exclaimed Caryn.

"Mr. Burger didn't seem to like us very much," said Violet.

"At first he was nice," Henry put in. "But all of a sudden, he just turned and walked away."

"Yes. We were telling him about Sunny being in the dog show and he looked really upset," said Violet.

Caryn shook her head. "Plum is a lovely, wonderful dog, but I'm afraid Lawrence Burger is just the opposite."

"What do you mean?" asked Henry.

"He only wants to win. He's jealous of anybody else who wins. He's particularly jealous of Sunny because Sunny and Plum are often finalists for the Best of Show."

"Does Sunny win?" asked Benny.

"Sometimes Sunny wins," answered Caryn. "Sometimes Plum does. Sometimes other dogs do. But you know what's sad? Even when Plum wins, Lawrence never seems to enjoy it."

"It *is* too bad," said Mrs. Teague. "But some dog show people are like that, unfortunately."

"They think winning is everything?" asked Grandfather Alden.

"Exactly," said Mrs. Teague.

Caryn laughed softly. "I like winning, and so does Sunny. But I think Sunny likes other things, also."

"Like bones," guessed Benny.

"And playing," said Violet.

"And sleeping in the sun," suggested Jessie.

"Yes, all of those things — things I bet Plum likes, too. I hope someday Lawrence learns to enjoy life with Plum, instead of always worrying about winning," Mrs. Teague said.

"I hope so, too," said Benny.

Caryn smiled. "Well, it's time for Sunny to go to bed. It's a big day tomorrow and she needs her rest. And so do I!"

"So do we all," said Grandfather Alden, standing up. "Time for bed."

"I hope tomorrow hurries up and gets here," said Violet.

"It will be here soon, Violet," promised Grandfather Alden.

The next day, everyone in the Alden house was up early. The Teagues and Sunny left first. "We have to get to the benching area by eight-thirty," explained Caryn as they loaded Sunny and her equipment for the dog show into the car.

"We'll see you there *very* soon," Benny promised.

The Alden children hurried through breakfast. Then Grandfather drove them all to the Greenfield Center.

The center was even busier and more full of dogs than it had been the day before. The sound of barking filled the air. The loud-speaker boomed overhead. People hurried by in all kinds of clothes — some in aprons with pockets that held scissors and brushes, others in suits.

"The people in the aprons must be groomers," said Henry. "Caryn was explaining that they often work on combing and clipping the dogs to make them look as good as possible, right up to the moment they go in the ring!"

"That's a lot of work," Jessie said.

Henry explained more as they walked through the center. "There are rules about how dogs can be cut for the shows, too."

"It's funny, isn't it?" Violet gave a little skip. "Dogs get haircuts just like people do!"

Grandfather said, "Here are your ticket stubs. Our seats are in the middle over there. I'm going to buy a program for us and sit down. After you've looked around a little, why don't you come join me?"

"Okay, Grandfather," said Henry. "I'll put the tickets in my pocket where I can't lose them."

Grandfather went to find their seats around the show ring, while Henry, Jessie,

Violet, and Benny walked toward the benching area.

"Look, there's Mrs. DeCicco," said Henry. "Let's go say hello and wish her luck."

But as the Aldens got closer, they saw that Mrs. DeCicco was talking to three people wearing suits.

"Maybe we can wish her luck another time," said Violet shyly. Before the Aldens could leave, however, Mrs. DeCicco saw them and motioned them to come over.

"These are the Alden children, who helped me with my beagles last night when Ruth didn't show up. And these" — Mrs. DeCicco clasped her hands and almost bowed — "are some of the judges! They are some of *the* most important people at a dog show."

"Oh, now, I wouldn't say that," the tallest judge put in with a little shake of her head. "I'd say the owners and the handlers — and the dogs themselves — are the most important part of the show."

Mrs. DeCicco unclasped her hands and

wagged her finger. "No, no! Don't you believe it, children. These are *wonderful* judges.
You know, I've been at shows where I've felt
that the judges just didn't understand what
a good beagle is. And of course my babies
are perfect examples!" Mrs. DeCicco
laughed and patted the tall judge's arm. The
judge, looking uncomfortable, took a step
backward as Mrs. DeCicco went on. "I
know I can rely on you to choose the *best*
dog."

All of the judges looked a little embar-
rassed at Mrs. DeCicco's gushing words.
The tall judge cleared her throat and said,
"We do our best." She turned to the Aldens.
"Are you enjoying the dog show?"

The Alden children all smiled politely.
"It's our first dog show," said Jessie. "We're
having a lot of fun!"

The judges all smiled. "I'm glad," said the
tall judge.

"Good luck to you, Mrs. DeCicco," said
another judge, and the three judges moved
away down the benching aisle.

As the judges left, Mrs. DeCicco nervously clasped her hands again. "Judges!" she said. "Oh, dear, oh dear."

"Is Ruth still missing?" asked Henry.

"What? Oh, no. She got here late last night. She'd had a flat tire. Strangest thing, you know. She'd just put new tires on her car." Mrs. DeCicco kept staring in the direction the judges had gone. "Oh, dear," she repeated. "I must win. I *must*."

"Mrs. DeCicco?" said Violet. "Winning isn't everything."

Mrs. DeCicco looked at Violet. "Maybe not. But if I don't win, I could lose everything!"

"What do you mean?" asked Jessie.

"I've put all my money, everything, into my beagles. And they all used to win all the time. But then I was in an accident and couldn't show my dogs for a long time. Now we have to start winning again soon, or I won't have any money left. I'll be forced to sell my dogs and my kennel!"

"Oh, dear," said Violet.

"I'm sure your beagles will win," said Henry.

With a sad, serious expression, Mrs. DeCicco said, "Do you think so? I hope you're right. They're such good dogs." She turned toward the three kennels with her beagles lined up inside. She bent down, and the sad expression left her face. "Aren't my beagles good boys and girls?"

The beagles began to bark happily. "Yes, *good* dogs, the best beagles in the world, no matter what," Mrs. DeCicco told them.

Henry looked at his watch. "We still have time to look around some more," he said. After saying good-bye to Mrs. DeCicco, the Aldens made their way through the benching area, still staring at all the different kinds of dogs and all their amazing shapes and sizes and colors.

Then Jessie said, "Look!"

At the very end of the row, a man was sneaking up to an unguarded kennel. He kept looking back over his shoulder nervously as he bent down. Inside the kennel, the Aldens could see a droopy-jowled basset hound growling angrily.

"Nice dog," said the man. The dog kept

growling, watching the man suspiciously.

"Good doggie," said the man. He appeared to be fumbling with the latch on the kennel door. The dog raised itself up on its front legs and barked. The man jerked his hand back.

"Excuse me," said Henry.

The man jumped and spun around. He was not much taller than Henry. He had brown wispy hair combed across the top of his almost bald head, heavy brown eyebrows, and sharp little blue eyes.

"Excuse me," Henry repeated. "Could we help you?"

"No!" said the man hastily. "Why do you ask?"

"Is that your basset hound?" asked Jessie.

"Why?" the man said.

"Because he doesn't seem to know you. If you were his owner, I don't think he'd bark at you like that," persisted Jessie.

"Okay, okay, so the dog isn't mine. A man can look at another person's dog, can't he?

It's a free country! Besides, I'm thinking of buying one. Yeah, that's it. Maybe this one. Now, if you kids will excuse me — " With that, the man pushed past the Aldens and disappeared into the crowd!

# CHAPTER 6

# A Bad Haircut

The Aldens stared as the strange man hurried away.

"Do you think he was trying to steal that dog?" asked Violet.

Jessie put her hands on her hips. "I don't know. It sure looked like it. But how could he, in the middle of a dog show with so many people around?"

"With so many people, it might be easier," suggested Henry. "Everybody is busy with their own dog and not paying attention to other people's dogs. And there are so many

people and so many dogs, no one really
knows which person goes with which dog."

"I never thought about that," Jessie said
thoughtfully. Violet and Benny nodded in
agreement.

Just then, an announcement came over the
loudspeaker: "Attention! The First Annual
Greenfield Dog Show is about to begin!"

"We'd better hurry!" exclaimed Henry.
The children walked hastily back through
the benching area and went to join their
grandfather. Mrs. Teague was already there
with Grandfather Alden. Through binoculars, she was watching all the different breeds
of dogs that were to be shown being led first
into the arena and then to their show rings.

"Just in time," Grandfather said.

"Aren't you supposed to be with Sunny?"
Violet asked as they all took their seats.

Mrs. Teague lowered her binoculars and
leaned back. "I'll go to ringside when her
breed, the golden retrievers, is about to be
judged. Meanwhile, I'm going to enjoy the
dog show from here, with all of you!"

Although they had already seen many,

many kinds of dogs in the benching area, the Aldens were amazed to see even more breeds of dogs being led into the rings. Mrs. Teague explained about all the different breeds and told them stories about some of the dogs she knew. One dog had saved her master's life by waking him up when a fire started in the hotel where he was staying. Another dog made visits to children who were sick in the hospital.

The Aldens watched and listened and applauded. At last it was time for the golden retrievers. Mrs. Teague hurried down to the ring as the beautiful golden dogs were being led in.

"Look, there's Caryn!" cried Jessica.

Caryn was wearing pants and a jacket that exactly matched Sunny's coat. She had on flat black shoes and a soft white blouse, and her golden hair was pulled back with a red bow.

"Caryn's all dressed up," Benny said. "She's as pretty as Sunny!"

The other Aldens laughed and Benny

laughed, too, although he wasn't sure why everyone was laughing.

The judge made a motion, and the handlers led their dogs in a circle around the ring. Then they all stopped at one side.

When the judge signaled, each handler and dog came forward, one pair at a time. The judge looked in each dog's mouth and ears and ran her hands over the dog's body. Afterwards, the handler walked the dog around the ring while the judge studied the way the dog moved and acted.

When Sunny's turn came, she stood proudly, her tail wagging slightly while the judge examined her. As Caryn led her in a circle around the ring, the Aldens clapped and cheered.

"I hope she wins," said Henry.

"She's the best dog, no matter what," said Violet loyally.

One by one the judge eliminated all the dogs except Sunny and a male golden retriever.

"He's a champion, too," said Jessie, studying her program.

The other dog finished his circle of the ring. Now the two dogs stood at attention at the side of the ring. The judge rubbed her chin. She walked back and forth between the two dogs. Then she made a motion for the dogs to walk around the ring again.

The two handlers led their dogs in a circle once more. As they passed the judge, she held up one finger to signal number 1, and pointed to Sunny, then two fingers and pointed to the other dog.

"Sunny won!" cried Henry.

"Hooray, hooray!" Benny shouted. They applauded as the judge handed a big blue ribbon to Caryn. Photographers took pictures of the new Greenfield Dog Show Champion Golden Retriever from every angle.

The Aldens watched as Caryn led Sunny out of the ring. Mrs. Teague hugged Caryn first, and then Sunny.

"Let's go down and meet the Teagues and

Sunny in the benching area," suggested Grandfather Alden.

"Oh, boy," said Benny. Hopping up and down with excitement, he led the way out of the viewing stands and back to the benching area where the golden retrievers were staying.

On their way, they saw two familiar faces. "Woof," said a friendly dog voice.

"Oh, it's Plum," said Violet, reaching out to pat the eager sheepdog's head.

"Congratulations," said an icy voice that didn't sound as if it meant the word at all.

At the other end of Plum's leash stood Lawrence Burger. "I see your little friend Sunny won," he said.

"Thank you," said Jessie politely.

"I hope Plum wins, too," said Benny.

Lawrence Burger smiled a cold smile. "Do you? Somehow, I doubt that. Come along, Plum."

The two walked away.

"What a strange man," said Henry. "Come on, let's go find Sunny — "

Just then, there was a horrible shriek.

Everyone stopped and turned to stare in the direction of the sound.

A man came running by, leading a big white poodle on a leash. "Look! Look what someone has done to my beautiful Curly!" he shrieked.

"Oh, look," gasped Violet. "Poor dog!"

Curly's beautiful, curly white coat had been shaved into ragged stripes.

A dog show official came hurrying up with a security guard. The security guard began to ask the man questions while the official tried to calm him down.

"I don't know *when* it happened," the man said. "I took Curly to have a little touch-up grooming, just after he won the poodle competition. Then I got a message that I had a phone call. But when I got to the information booth, there was no one on the phone. I was on my way back when I met my groomer going to the information booth. He said *he'd* gotten an urgent message to meet me there. I told him I never sent such a message. When we got back, we found Curly on the grooming table — like *this*!"

"Have you noticed any suspicious characters hanging around your dog?" asked the security guard.

"There's a suspicious character!" Henry nudged Jessie. Sure enough, there was the man they had seen near the basset hound's kennel. As they watched, the man disappeared into the crowd.

"No," moaned Curly's owner. "I didn't notice anyone suspicious. "Oh, this is awful. Now Curly's chances of winning the Best in Show are ruined. *Ruined*!"

"Look, Mrs. DeCicco," cried Benny, as Mrs. DeCicco passed nearby. "Look at Curly!"

But Mrs. DeCicco didn't seem to hear Benny or notice the poodle. She walked right by, as if she didn't want to be connected to the incident in any way.

"That's odd," said Jessie. But before she could say anything else, Grandfather said, "We'd better go find the Teagues and Sunny."

By the time the Aldens joined them, the

Teagues had already heard about what had happened. Sunny was lying in her kennel, which had a big blue ribbon fastened to it, eating a dog biscuit and looking unconcerned. But Mrs. Teague and Caryn were plainly shocked.

"Who would do such an awful thing?" asked Caryn.

"And why?" asked Henry.

"Maybe it was a joke," Benny suggested. He added, "A *bad* joke."

"Whoever did it was a bad person, Benny," said Jessie. "But I don't think it was a joke."

"Maybe someone did it to eliminate the competition. You know, if Curly can't compete, maybe someone else has a better chance of winning," said Violet.

Henry nodded. "Yes! Maybe the person whose poodle came in second did it. That makes them first now, doesn't it?"

"I'm not sure." Caryn frowned. "But the poodle who came in second, the reserve champion, is owned by a very honest woman. I'm sure she would never do something like that. She's a good person, and she loves dogs."

"That's true," Mrs. Teague said. She shook her head and sighed. "Oh, well. I suppose on the bright side of things, Curly will get a little vacation now while his coat grows back. He's been a show dog for a long time and has won almost everything a dog can win. Maybe he'll like getting to stay at home and enjoy a different life."

The Alden children exchanged glances. They were all remembering the couple they had overheard arguing the first day of the show. And they were all wondering if shaving Curly was the sort of thing someone would do because they believed dogs shouldn't be in dog shows.

"Could it have been that woman who was arguing that her dog Zonker should be allowed to quit being a show dog?" asked Jessie aloud.

"Or Mr. Burger?" suggested Violet. "He's such a mean man."

"He can't be all mean, can he?" asked Henry. "Or how could he have a dog as nice as Plum?"

Jessie lowered her voice. "What if it was Mrs. DeCicco? She really needs to win badly. And she was *right there*."

"I can't believe Mrs. DeCicco would do something like that!" exclaimed Violet.

"Time to go," said Grandfather Alden. He turned to Mrs. Teague. "But we'll be back tomorrow to see Sunny win again!"

"Is the Best Dog in Show contest tomorrow, Grandfather?" asked Benny as they left the Greenfield Center.

"No, that's the night after tomorrow, Benny," Grandfather explained. "Remember when Caryn said that all the breeds of dogs are divided into seven different groups?"

Benny looked puzzled.

"Sunny is in the Sporting Dog group, remember?" Jessie said.

"Y-yes." Benny still looked as puzzled as he sounded.

"Well, tomorrow Sunny will compete against the other sporting dogs to see who is the very best sporting dog."

"Oh," said Benny. "I think I see . . . when Sunny wins tomorrow, will she be the best sporting dog at the dog show?"

"Yes, Benny!" Henry said. "Then, the next night, the best dog in each group — Herding, Sporting, Working, Terrier, Hound, Non-sporting and Toy — will compete to see who is the best dog in the *whole* show."

"Okay," said Benny. He gave a little skip. "Can we come see Sunny win tomorrow night and the next night, too?"

Grandfather Alden laughed, but before he could answer, they saw Plum and his owner again.

"Oh, look," said Violet. "Plum won the blue ribbon!"

Sure enough, Mr. Burger was holding a blue ribbon and looking very pleased.

"Congratulations!" called Jessie.

"Thank you!" said Mr. Burger. Then he

saw who had said it, and his smile froze. He turned on his heel and marched Plum in the other direction.

Watching them go, Violet shook her head. "I don't like Mr. Burger very much. But *Plum* is a nice dog."

# CHAPTER 7

# A Surprise for Sunny

"I want to make a surprise for Sunny," announced Benny the next morning after the Aldens and the Teagues had finished breakfast and Grandfather had taken the Teagues on a tour of Greenfield. Benny and his brother and two sisters had gone to their boxcar. Violet and Henry were sweeping it out and dusting it while Jessie and Benny oiled a squeaky hinge on the boxcar door and fixed a rickety leg on the table.

"A surprise, Benny? What kind of a surprise?" asked Violet.

"Something special for when Sunny wins the whole show," Benny told her. He frowned, thinking hard. "Maybe a chocolate cake."

Henry laughed and shook his head. "Sunny might like chocolate cake, Benny, but I don't think it would be very good for her."

"Oh, yes," said Benny. "I remember Mrs. Teague telling us that chocolate could make dogs very, very sick." His eyes widened at the awful thought of not being able to eat chocolate.

Violet had been thinking hard, too. Suddenly she clapped her hands together. "I know! We could make a flag for Sunny, or a banner, to wave at the show for her when she wins!"

Benny clapped his hands together, too. "Yes! A beautiful, *big* banner!"

Violet reached up and pulled a shoebox off one of the shelves in the boxcar. "We still have paints in here from the time we made signs for our helper service," she said. She studied the contents of the box thoughtfully and said, "But not enough to make a really *great* banner."

"Well, we're almost finished here," said Henry. "As soon as we do, let's ride our bicycles into town and get some more art supplies."

"Good idea," said Jessie. She checked the leg on the table one last time to make sure that it wasn't loose anymore and then stood up. "We can get a long roll of paper for the banner."

"We need some way to hold it up, too," said Violet. "Maybe a stick or pole — sort of like a short flagpole — at each end, so we can raise it up high."

Henry added, "Yes, and we could roll the banner up from each end, then. That would make it easy to carry without tearing it."

"I get to hold one end of the banner, don't I?" demanded Benny.

"You and I will hold one end, Benny, and Violet and Jessie can hold the other," answered Henry.

"Okay," Benny agreed.

As quickly as they could, the Aldens finished their work in the boxcar. Soon they were on their bicycles riding into town to get supplies to make a banner for Sunny.

In the art supply store, they found just the right roll of paper for making a long banner. Benny picked out some gold paint for writing Sunny's name on the banner. "It sort of matches her coat," he explained.

But they couldn't find poles to attach to the ends of the banner.

"Why don't you try the hardware store," suggested the owner of the art supply store. "Maybe a yardstick would be just the thing."

"A yardstick! That might work. Thank you," said Henry.

Carrying their supplies, the Aldens went into the hardware store. Inside, they found all kinds of sticks and poles, flat and round, used for building things. "This is great," said Jessie holding up a thin, smooth, round wooden pole that was almost as long as she was tall. "It's called a *dowel*. I wonder what it is used for?"

"I don't know, but look at this green pole. It's used for staking up tomatoes and peas and beans in gardens," said Henry.

"Both of those would work," said Violet.

"Here are the yardsticks!" cried Benny. He held up two yardsticks, with the flat sides marked out into feet and inches. "Why are they called yardsticks?"

"Because they are three feet long. That's a yard," explained Violet.

"Oh," said Benny. He waved the sticks. "I like these. Let's use the yardsticks."

"It would probably be easier to attach the banners to the flat sides of the yardstick," said Jessie, putting the dowels down reluctantly.

"True," said Henry. "Yardsticks it is, Benny."

"Good." Still holding the yardsticks up high, Benny led the way down the aisle to the cash register. But at the end of the aisle he stopped and pointed one of the yardsticks in front of him. "Look," he whispered loudly. "There's the polka-dot woman! The one with the dog named Zonker!"

Sure enough, ahead of them at the counter was the woman who owned Zonker. Today

They all laughed. Just then, they heard Mrs. McGregor's voice. "Lunchtime!" she called.

"We'll put the yardsticks on when it's dry, after lunch," said Jessie.

"It's a beautiful poster," said Benny. "See? I even put gold stars around Sunny and Watch."

"It *is* a beautiful poster, Benny," said Violet.

Pleased with their morning's work, the Aldens hurried back to the house to wash their hands and have their lunch.

CHAPTER 8

# An Unexpected Visitor

At last it was evening, time to go to the dog show. The Aldens had finished the banner and put it carefully away, until the next night when they felt sure Sunny would compete for Best in Show. Then they'd gotten dressed up and gone to the Center. They saw that everyone else was dressed up for the evening's judging, too. Some of the handlers were wearing long dresses or dark suits. One man even had on a tuxedo. Excitement was in the air.

*81*

Mrs. DeCicco was dressed up, too. She was wearing a short, glittery dress with silvery high-heeled shoes.

"You look great, Mrs. DeCicco," Benny told her.

Mrs. DeCicco seemed startled for a moment as if she were surprised to see them. Then she smiled. "Thank you, Benny," she said. "I think this dress will stand out in the show ring, don't you? It doesn't hurt to catch the judge's attention, you know."

"Why are you carrying scissors?" asked Benny.

"Scissors?" Mrs. DeCicco looked down at the small scissorlike instrument in her hand.

"Oh!" exclaimed Violet. "Those aren't scissors, are they? They're grooming clippers. Remember, the groomer who was working on Curly had grooming clippers just like that."

"Do you trim the beagles?" asked Jessie. "They don't seem to have much hair to trim."

Mrs. DeCicco looked startled again, and then a little uncomfortable and embarrassed. "Well," she said, "Er, actually, don't tell anyone, but I was just on my way to do a little trimming on my own hair. My bangs are a little too long, and these are much sharper than ordinary scissors, you know! I keep them just for me." With an embarrassed little laugh, she waved and left.

"Euuw," said Jessie. "Dog scissors!"

"She just uses them for her own hair, Jessie. You heard her," Violet said. "She doesn't need them for the beagles."

"I think it's sort of suspicious, anyway," said Henry. "Maybe that's not why she has them at all."

"Do you think *she* was the one who clipped Curly?" asked Violet.

"I don't know," said Henry. "Maybe. . . ."

Just then, Grandfather said, "There's Mrs. Teague. Come on, everybody." The Alden children followed their grandfather into the stands to join their friend.

"Oh, look! We have ringside seats," said Jessie as the Aldens sat down. "This is great!"

Mrs. Teague nodded, looking pleased by Jessie's excitement. "They always give the winners the best seats for the final judgings."

"Thank you for inviting us," said Violet, and the others joined in with their appreciation.

"I'm glad you could be here," Mrs. Teague added. "It is wonderful for Sunny to have her own cheering section."

"Hooray for Sunny!" cried Benny.

Everyone laughed. "Not yet, Benny," said Jessie. "But soon."

"Look!" said Henry. "Here comes the first group of dogs."

"The terriers," said Mrs. Teague. She pointed to a small dog with a short tail and pointed face. "That's the fox terrier champion, called Chaser. He's favored to win the best of the terrier group."

"If he wins, that means he'll compete for best dog in the whole show, Benny," Violet explained.

Benny nodded seriously.

Even the judges were more dressed up that night. The judge of the terrier group had on a tuxedo with a red cummerbund and a red bow tie. He had rosy cheeks and little round glasses that he kept pushing up on his short, turned-up nose.

The dogs walked into the ring. An expectant hush fell over the audience.

Suddenly Chaser lunged to the end of his leash and began barking hysterically!

The square black Scottish terrier next to him did the same thing!

Then all the dogs began to jump and bark. One dog pulled loose from her handler and ran across the ring, knocking over a small table before anyone could catch her. Two other dogs got their leashes tangled as they leaped and struggled to get free. Shouts of surprise filled the Greenfield Center.

"Oh no!" cried Violet. "Look!"

A very frightened black-and-white spotted cat was dodging across the arena, skittering away from each dog, and from the people who were now trying to catch him.

"Look over there! By the entrance! Isn't that the same man we saw yesterday? At the basset hound cage?" said Henry.

"Where? I don't see anyone," said Jessie.

"Come on!" said Henry as the cat darted

between the legs of the officials. "That cat needs help!"

The Alden children jumped out of their seats and hurried to the stairs leading to the arena floor.

The small black-and-white form streaked by.

"He's heading for the benching area!" gasped Henry. "We'd better catch him before he gets back there."

The children raced down the corridor just in time to see the cat dodge through an open door that said FIRST AID. A young man in a white coat who had been sitting by the door jumped up in surprise.

"Was that a *cat*?" he asked in amazement.

"Yes," panted Violet. "We have to catch him."

"Quick, go inside!" said the young man. "I'll close the door!"

"Thanks," said Henry as the children hurried by the young man and into the small first aid room.

Benny bent down and looked under the narrow bed on one side of the room. "There he is. He's hiding under the bed."

"Oh, poor kitty," said Violet. "He must be so scared. We should be very quiet and let him calm down."

The Aldens sat down on the floor, and Violet began to talk softly to the frightened cat. At last the cat let her reach under the bed and pick him up.

Violet looked puzzled. "You know, this cat looks like Spike — the cat we saw in the hardware store with the polka-dot woman."

"You're right!" exclaimed Henry.

Violet looked even more puzzled. "But how did he get loose at the dog show?"

"I don't know," said Henry, "but we'd better get him out of here now!"

Benny patted the cat's head.

"Oh, good, you caught him," said the young man. "I've been a nurse for a while now. But it's the first time I've ever had a cat in the first aid room!"

"What do we do now?" asked Benny.

"Maybe we should find the polka-dot woman, and ask her if this is her cat," said Jessie.

"Or we could take him to the Greenfield Animal Shelter," Violet suggested. "They'll know how to find his owner. He has a collar."

"But we can't go now," said Henry. "We have to see Sunny compete."

"I have an idea," Jessie said. "Wait here." She ran down the corridor toward the benching area. A few minutes later she hurried back, holding a small animal carrier. It had air holes in the side and a screen door that latched shut in the front.

"That's perfect," said Violet. "We can put the cat in here until after the show, then take it to the shelter."

"Where did you get the carrier?" asked Henry.

"Mrs. DeCicco," said Jessie, trying to catch her breath. "She said she just happened to have an extra one. I ran into her right outside. She said she always brings extra travel kennels for her beagles. She said we could bring it back tomorrow."

Carefully, Violet slipped the black-and-white cat into the carrier. Then they took the cat back with them and put the carrier on the floor at their feet.

"You did a good job," said Grandfather.

"Yes." Mrs. Teague smiled. "And you still have time to watch the judge finish the terrier group. It took a little while to get everyone settled down."

As the children watched, it became clear that some of the terriers were still upset by all the commotion caused by the cat. One small, bouncy terrier kept turning its head all around instead of looking straight ahead as it was led in a circle around the ring. Other terriers kept barking as they stood waiting their turn. The owners looked even more upset than the dogs. And Chaser kept pulling on his leash.

Mrs. Teague shook her head as she watched Chaser. "That's not good," she commented.

At last the judge chose the best of the terriers. But it wasn't Chaser. It was the white bull terrier who won.

There were gasps from the audience when the judge announced her choice. "It's an upset victory for the bull terrier," said Mrs. Teague.

"That's Shug!" said Violet. "Remember that bull terrier we met when we were walking Mrs. DeCicco's beagles?"

"Yes!" the other children said. They applauded as the terriers were led out of the ring.

When Sunny's turn came, they applauded even louder.

"How can the judge not see she's the very best!" whispered Violet.

"The other dogs are good, too," said Henry, trying to be fair.

It was true. The black labrador retriever was obviously a champion. He walked confidently around the ring, his head held high, causing the judge to nod approvingly. And a beautiful Irish setter with a gleaming red coat won a loud round of applause from the spectators.

"Oh, dear," said Violet. They all cheered extra loud when Sunny's turn came.

The judge motioned for the Sporting Group to circle once more. Then she had all the dogs line up again. Slowly, she walked up and down the line.

She stopped in front of the labrador.

She stopped in front of Sunny.

She stepped back and raised one finger for first place — and pointed at Sunny!

"She's going to win Best in Show! I just know it!" said Henry as Caryn and Sunny stood proudly in the center of the ring accepting their award.

"I think you're right," said Jessie.

At last the judging was over. The Aldens took the cat to the animal shelter, where the night attendant let them in.

"We'll take good care of him," the attendant promised. "Meanwhile, I bet he'd like some food and water, wouldn't you, fella?" He lifted the cat out of the carrier and handed the carrier to Jessie. Then, holding the cat in his arms and talking to him, the attendant carried him to the back of the shelter where the cats were kept.

"How do you think the cat got in the dog show?" asked Henry as Grandfather drove them home.

"I wouldn't go to a dog show if I was a cat," Benny said sleepily, leaning against Grandfather's shoulder.

"Do you think someone did it on purpose?" Violet wondered aloud. "Like that mean trick they played on Curly?"

"Well, however the cat got in the Greenfield Center, he sure upset all the terriers. Chaser, the dog favored to win, was so upset that he *didn't* win," Henry pointed out.

"Someone had to have let that cat in," agreed Jessie. "But who? And why?"

But no one could think of any answers.

CHAPTER 9

## Sunny Disappears

The next day, the last day of the Greenfield Dog Show, was bright and clear. Since Watch couldn't go to the dog show, and since he had to go to the veterinarian's that afternoon to get his shots (although of course, *he* didn't know it), the Aldens decided to take him for a special walk in the park. As Watch ran and sniffed happily, the four of them discussed all the mysterious things that had been happening.

"It's as if someone is trying to ruin the whole dog show," said Henry. "But why?"

They all watched silently for a moment as Watch sniffed at something under a tree. He cocked his head and started to dig furiously.

Then Jessie went on thoughtfully, "First we see that suspicious-looking man at the basset hound's cage, and he doesn't even have a good reason for being there . . ."

"And then someone shaves poor Curly the poodle," put in Violet.

Nodding, Jessie went on, "And that's when we saw that same man again."

"But we saw Mrs. DeCicco then, too. She pretended not to see us, remember?" said Henry.

"Maybe she really *didn't* see us," objected Violet. "She's got a lot on her mind."

"Maybe," said Henry doubtfully. "Anyway, don't forget that we also saw Mrs. DeCicco with those grooming scissors. It's hard to believe she'd really use them to trim her bangs."

"And she did have that extra carrier when the cat was let out," said Jessie.

"But it looked like that cat we saw with the polka-dot woman," said Benny.

"I know." Jessie bit her lower lip, thinking hard. "We called the shelter this morning. No one has claimed the cat yet, and we haven't seen the polka-dot woman to find out if that cat is hers."

"It could be," said Henry. "We heard her say she doesn't think Zonker should have to keep going to dog shows. So maybe she is trying to sabotage the whole dog show."

Jessie said, "That's true. Or maybe it's Mrs. DeCicco. Maybe she is trying to make sure she wins. She said she has to win or she'll lose everything."

"But she's so nice," said Violet.

"Remember that Great Dane?" asked Benny suddenly. "He looked mean, but he was nice. You said you can't tell by looking at someone."

"You're right, Benny." Violet sighed.

"What about Mr. Burger?" said Benny. He picked up a stick. "Here, Watch!" he called and threw the stick. Watch stopped digging and ran to look for the stick. "Mr. Burger's mean, and he thinks winning is the most important thing."

"Just because he's mean doesn't mean he'd sabotage a whole dog show," said Henry. "Besides, we haven't seen him around when any of this has been happening. And unlike Mrs. DeCicco, he's not going to lose *everything* if he loses."

"Don't forget the mysterious man, either," said Jessie. She paused, then added, "Maybe it is Mr. Burger! Maybe he and the mysterious man are working together!"

"Or the mysterious man and Mrs. DeCicco. Or the polka-dot woman," said Henry.

"Come on, Watch, time to go back," called Violet. The Aldens walked slowly through the park and back down the street. When they reached home, they were no nearer to solving the mystery.

That afternoon, before Watch's appointment, they went to the center to see how Sunny and Caryn were doing. The feeling of excitement that had been in the air the night before was even stronger.

"Let's find Caryn quick and wish her good luck," said Benny.

But before they could find Caryn, she found them.

"Caryn, what's wrong?" asked Jessie as Caryn hurried toward them.

"It's Sunny," gasped Caryn, her face pale. "She's gone!"

"*Gone?* What do you mean?" asked Henry.

Caryn took a deep breath to try and calm herself. But her voice was shaky as she answered, "She's disappeared. One minute she was in her kennel, with her chin on her favorite toy, and the next minute . . ."

"You mean she got out of her kennel?" asked Violet. "Is she lost?"

"No! At least, I don't think so." Caryn looked around as if Sunny might come walking toward them. "No, it's impossible for her to open her kennel by herself. Someone had to have let her out!"

"Another mean trick," gasped Violet.

Henry patted Caryn's hand. "She can't have gone far. Someone would have seen her wandering around and recognized her, wouldn't they?"

"I don't know," said Caryn. "My mother

and I asked everybody who'd been around us if they'd seen anything, but they're all so busy that no one was paying any attention. Mrs. DeCicco had stopped by to say hi a little earlier. She did say she thought she saw someone sort of hanging around nearby. But she can't remember what he looked like."

Caryn let go of Henry's arm and clasped her hands together. "Oh, dear, oh, dear. All I did was walk to the end of the aisle to fill Sunny's water dish. How could there have been time for her to get out? Or for someone to let her out!"

"We'll find her," said Henry reassuringly. "We can divide up and look."

Jessie and Benny, Violet and Henry, and Caryn all went to look for Sunny. But when the three search parties met back at Sunny's empty kennel half an hour later, no one had found her, or found anyone who remembered seeing her.

"Did she have on a collar?" asked Henry. "Maybe she got out of the center somehow and someone will find her around town."

"Sunny wasn't wearing a collar," said

Caryn. She seemed a little calmer, but she was still pale with worry. "She's been tatooed on her inner thigh with a registration number — many show dogs are — but I didn't have her collar on her."

Henry looked serious. "I guess some people wouldn't know to look for a registration number," he said.

"No, but every veterinarian does, and every animal shelter," said Caryn.

"Why don't we call the Greenfield Animal Shelter and see if they've found her?" suggested Violet.

"Good idea," said Henry. He hurried toward the phone booths. But he returned shortly, shaking his head. "No Sunny," he said. "I left a description in case anyone did turn in a lost golden retriever." He started to say something else, then stopped.

"I just remembered, we have to take Watch to Dr. Scott's," Jessie said.

"That's right," said Henry quickly. He looked at Caryn. "We have to go now," he said. "But we'll come back as soon as we can to help you keep looking."

Caryn smiled bravely. "Thank you," she said. "I'd better go file a report."

"See you in a little while," said Henry.

"We'll find Sunny. I know we will," Violet told Caryn.

As the Aldens hurried home, Henry said, "I didn't want to say anything in front of Caryn, but when I called the shelter, I was told that someone had claimed the black-and-white cat."

"Who?" asked Benny.

"A very angry woman. And she was wearing — "

"Black-and-white spots," guessed Jessie.

"Right," said Henry. "She told the attendant at the animal shelter that someone had *stolen* the cat out of her hotel room last night while she and her husband and Zonker were at the dog show."

"Wow," said Violet softly.

The Aldens were quiet as they got Watch and walked to Dr. Scott's office. At last Benny broke the silence. "Do you think someone stole Sunny, too? Do you think there's a petnapper?"

Jessie looked grim. "It sure seems that way."

"Mrs. DeCicco? She was right there," said Henry.

"Not Mrs. DeCicco," cried Violet. She put her hands in her pockets and shook her head.

"But she's been around when everything has happened. And don't you think it is a little suspicious that she just happened to have an extra carrier with her? Maybe that's what she used to bring the cat into the show in the first place," reasoned Henry.

They turned the corner and walked down the road to the veterinarian's.

"I think it was the suspicious man," said Violet. "He was outside the basset hound's kennel. Maybe he was going to steal the basset hound, and instead he stole Sunny!"

"But then why would he bring a cat into the show? Or shave Curly?" asked Jessie.

"I don't know," said Violet, wrinkling her brow. "Could it be the polka-dot woman? Would she be mean enough to let her own cat loose at a dog show?"

"It's mean Mr. Burger," insisted Benny. "I don't like him."

Hearing the tone of Benny's voice, Watch barked in agreement and pulled on his leash.

"Whoa, boy," said Violet.

"Just because you don't like someone doesn't mean he's bad, Benny. But you're right to suspect him, I think," said Jessie. "He wants to win. With Sunny out of the way, his chances are better." She added thoughtfully, "So are Mrs. DeCicco's."

"It really is almost like someone is trying to sabotage the Greenfield Dog Show," said Henry.

"Maybe that is it," said Violet.

"All the bad luck things that have been happening *have* happened to the whole dog show. But why would anyone want to ruin a dog show?" asked Jessie.

"Maybe it's someone who doesn't like dogs," Benny said.

"Here's Dr. Scott's office," said Violet.

Watch knew where he was. His ears went down and his tail drooped. He planted all four feet firmly on the sidewalk and refused to move. At last Violet had to bend over, pick him up, and carry him inside.

Dr. Scott smiled kindly when she saw Watch. "There's a good boy," she said, checking him out. The way she looked in his mouth and ears and ran her hands over him was sort of the same way the judge handled dogs in the show.

"Now," said Dr. Scott, "who will hold Watch while I give him his shots?"

Benny closed his eyes shut and grabbed Violet's hand. Soft-hearted Violet shook her head and looked away.

"Henry and I will," said Jessie.

"Hang on now," Dr. Scott said.

But it turned out they didn't have to hold on tight at all. Dr. Scott was such a good veterinarian that Watch hardly seemed to feel his shots.

Very soon Dr. Scott said, "All done."

Benny opened his eyes and they all began to pet and praise Watch, telling him what a good, brave dog he was.

"Here," said Dr. Scott. She reached in a jar on the counter and pulled out a small dog biscuit. Jessie lifted Watch down onto the floor, and Dr. Scott gave him the biscuit. He munched on it happily.

As Watch ate his biscuit, the Aldens asked Dr. Scott about her vacation.

"It was a good vacation," Dr. Scott told them. "But I'm glad to be back. What's been happening while I was away?"

"The dog show!" exclaimed Benny. He pulled on Dr. Scott's sleeve. "May I go visit the dogs who are staying with you?"

"Yes, Benny, you may," said Dr. Scott. "My assistant is back there now."

"Thank you," said Benny, and he went to visit the dogs.

Dr. Scott turned to Jessie, Violet, and Henry. "I have tickets for tonight," said Dr. Scott. "Do you like dog shows?"

"We have one of the dogs staying with us," said Jessie. "Or we used to, until she disappeared!"

"Disappeared?" asked Dr. Scott. "What happened?"

So the Aldens told Dr. Scott all about Sunny and how she had disappeared from the dog show that morning, and about all the other mysterious things that had happened.

"I don't know. It could be that someone *is* trying to sabotage the dog show," Dr. Scott said thoughtfully. "Although I can't imagine why. Whatever is going on, someone is up to no good!"

"We've got to find Sunny," said Henry. "So she can win best in show tonight."

"But we don't know where else to look — " began Violet.

"Sunny, Sunny, Sunny!" cried Benny. He came barreling back into the examining room and skidded to a stop. He pointed back toward Dr. Scott's kennels. "Sunny is back there!"

"Benny, it can't be Sunny. What would she be doing at Dr. Scott's?" asked Henry.

"It is Sunny, it is," insisted Benny. "I knew who she was and she knew me, too!"

Jessie shook her head. "I know you want to find Sunny as badly as the rest of us do, Benny, but. . . ."

"Do you have a golden retriever staying with you, Dr. Scott?" Violet asked.

"As a matter of fact someone just brought one in," Dr. Scott said. "Would you like to see her?"

"It's Sunny," Benny said stubbornly.

"Come on, Benny. We'll all go see," said Violet.

Swallowing the last bit of his biscuit, Watch trotted after them, with Henry holding his leash. But when they got to the kennels, Watch barked excitedly and pulled the leash out of Henry's hand. He raced up to one of the dog runs and began pawing at the gate. On the other side of the gate, a beautiful golden retriever began barking and pawing, too.

"I don't believe it," said Henry. "Could that be Sunny?"

"Sunny," said Violet as they went up to the gate. "Sunny?"

The golden retriever leaped up excitedly.

"A man brought her in this morning," said Dr. Scott.

"Can you describe him?" asked Jessie.

"He was round. He had sort of shaggy gray hair, and it looked as if he had slept in his clothes, they were so wrinkled. That's really all I remember, but I would know him if I saw him again. He signed his name as Mr. Smith. He just wanted to board her overnight," said Dr. Scott, sounding puzzled.

"That sounds like . . . Mr. Burger!" said Henry.

"Does this dog have a tattoo?" asked Violet, pointing to the dog's inner thigh.

"Why, yes. I wrote it down on her forms when she was checked in." Dr. Scott paused to think.

"Do you know how to find out who she is registered to?" asked Henry.

"Yes, of course," said Dr. Scott. "There's a number you can call."

"Sunny is registered to Mrs. Annabel Teague," said Jessie.

Turning, Dr. Scott said, "I'm going to check this out right now. Wait here, please!"

A few minutes later the veterinarian came briskly back. "Sure enough — Annabel Teague is the owner," she said.

"It *is* Sunny! I knew it, I knew it!" Benny

jumped up and down with excitement.

"Good work, Benny," said Jessie. "I'm sorry I didn't believe you."

"That's okay. Watch believed me, didn't you Watch? Good boy!" Benny hugged the dog.

"We'd better call Caryn and tell her the good news," said Violet.

"Yes, and she can come pick up Sunny!" said Jessie.

"Wait a minute," said Henry. "Let *me* call Caryn. I have an idea. A way we could catch the person who did this!"

"What is it?" asked Jessie.

"Let me talk to Caryn about my idea," said Henry. "If she agrees, I'll tell you all about it."

And he hurried off to call Caryn with the good news about Sunny — and his mysterious idea.

# CHAPTER 10

# And the Winner Is . . .

At last it was evening, and the contest the Best of Show, the best dog at the First Annual Greenfield Dog Show, was about to begin. In their ringside seats, the Aldens and Mrs. Teague leaned forward eagerly.

One by one the seven dogs were led into the center of the arena. As each dog walked in, the crowd cheered wildly. Every dog was a champion, even if it didn't win Best of Show.

Lawrence Burger walked into the ring

with Plum at his side. He had a confident, superior little smile on his face. Beside him, Plum looked every inch a winner.

The Aldens applauded with the rest of the crowd, not for Lawrence Burger, but for his dog.

Mr. Burger took up his place in the ring and turned to face the center.

There was a pause. Then Caryn, dressed in a long glittery skirt and a silky blouse, led Sunny into the ring.

The crowd cheered. The Aldens cheered loudest of all.

Then Violet touched Jessie's arm to get her attention. "Look at Mr. Burger!"

Lawrence Burger wasn't cheering. His face was turning red. He looked like he was about to explode.

"It can't be," he cried. "That dog *can't* be here. I know because I left her at — "

Suddenly he stopped, his mouth open, his face even redder.

"What did you say?" asked the judge. She walked over and stood in front of Lawrence Burger.

"Nothing . . . I mean . . ."

The judge held up her hand. Several officials and other judges hurried into the ring. They took Caryn and Sunny, and Lawrence Burger and Plum off to one side while the crowd buzzed with astonished talk.

The Aldens quickly went to join Caryn and Sunny. Dr. Scott left her seat across the arena and came down into the ring, too.

"I would like an explanation of what is going on at *once*," said the judge sternly.

Lawrence Burger opened and closed his mouth like a fish gasping for air.

"We can explain," said Jessie, stepping forward.

"You? What do you know about this?" asked an official.

"A great deal," said Caryn. "They're the ones who found Sunny — and solved the mystery of why everything seemed to be going wrong at this dog show."

"Very well," said the judge. "Go ahead."

The Aldens took turns explaining all of the things that had gone wrong at the dog show. Then Dr. Scott identified Lawrence Burger as the man who had brought Sunny into her office to board her that morning, signing his name as Mr. Smith. When they had finished, the judge turned to face Lawrence Burger. "Did you do all those things?" she asked.

The proud, unpleasant look had left Lawrence Burger's face. Now he just looked miserable. "Yes," he confessed. "It was me. I shaved Curly so he wouldn't be able to compete for Best of Show. I knew that the dog favored to win the terrier group hated cats, so I — borrowed — that cat and turned it loose in the show. I even let out the air in the tires on Mrs. DeCicco's assistant's car. I hoped it would upset her and her dogs so much that they wouldn't do well. And I — borrowed — Sunny and took her to this veterinarian's office. I was going to go get her tomorrow morning and bring her back, honestly."

The judge shook her head. "This is bad, very bad." She and the other judges and officials stepped to one side and talked among themselves for a few minutes. Then the judge came back. "You are officially disqualified from this show. And you may be barred from showing dogs for a long time to come. You have disgraced the world of dog shows. And you have disgraced a fine dog. Your dog might well have won, fair and square. Now he may never get the chance to win again. You are dismissed."

His head hanging, Lawrence Burger walked miserably out of the ring. As they left, Plum licked his hand as if to try and comfort him. Mr. Burger looked down at Plum, stroked his head, then covered his eyes and hurried out of sight.

A few minutes later, the Reserve Champion was led into the arena to take Plum's place. The contest for Best in Show began.

It seemed to take the judge forever to look at each dog.

"I wish the judge would hurry up and decide," whispered Violet.

Mrs. Teague pressed her hand to her chest. "So do I!"

Henry leaned forward. "She *must* see that Caryn and Sunny are the best."

"Oh, I hope so!" said Jessie.

"Go, go, go, Sunny," said Benny.

At last the judge signaled for the seven dogs to circle the arena once more. And once again, the crowd cheered and cheered for the seven champions. Then the cheers rose to a thunder pitch as the judge pointed, 1,2,3,4 for the dogs that won first, second, third, and fourth.

"She won! She won!" cried Henry, jumping up.

"HOORAY FOR SUNNY!" shouted Benny.

All of the Aldens began to hug each other and Mrs. Teague, who was dabbing at her eyes with her sleeve. "Oh, I am so proud of Caryn and of Sunny," she kept saying. "So proud of them both!"

"They're real champions," Jessie said. "Even after everything that happened, they went out and won."

"Yes," agreed Mrs. Teague. "Oh, yes."

"Oh, good!" said Violet. "I was so excited that I almost didn't realize it, but Mrs. DeCicco's beagle Gloria came in second!"

"I'm so glad," said Jessie wholeheartedly.

"Let's go see everyone," said Benny, bouncing out of his seat.

"Okay, Benny," said Grandfather Alden. Together the Aldens and Mrs. Teague made their way through the excited crowd toward Sunny and Caryn.

"Congratulations!" called Violet as they passed Mrs. DeCicco, who was posing with Gloria for the photographers.

"Thank you!" answered Mrs. DeCicco, beaming. She kissed the top of Gloria's head and Gloria licked Mrs. DeCicco's face.

"Great shot," said one of the photographers, and everyone laughed. A moment later, they joined the Teagues and Sunny.

Just then, a familiar couple went by. "Come on, Zonker," said the polka-dot woman to the dalmatian at her side. "Time to go home."

The man beside her said, "You know, after this show, I think you're right. Maybe we all need a vacation."

The woman smiled.

"Oh, good," said Violet softly.

"Henry, Jessica, Violet, Benny — come

have your photograph taken with us. After all, if it hadn't been for you, Sunny wouldn't have been in the show at all!" Caryn said.

"Wait a minute!" cried Benny. "We *forgot*! We forgot the surprise!" He ran back to their seats.

"What surprise?" Caryn asked.

"You'll see," promised Henry as Benny came running back with the banner under his arm. Quickly, the Aldens unfurled the banner and held it up.

Caryn laughed with delight. "It's *wonderful*. Come on, let's all have our picture taken with it!"

As the Aldens joined the Teagues and Sunny, a young man came up to them. "It's a real scoop," he said. "What a story! How about an exclusive interview?"

"Well," said Jessie. Then she stopped. Her eyes widened. "I don't believe it!" she said. "What are *you* doing here?"

"I'm a reporter," said the man.

The Aldens all stared. It was the same man they had seen at the basset hound's cage, and lurking in the background when Curly had

been shaved, and near the entrance where the cat had first been seen at the show.

"A reporter," repeated Violet. "But what were you doing at the basset hound's cage? And when Curly got shaved — you were right there!"

"Yes," said Jessie. "And you were right there when the cat got in, too!"

The reporter shrugged. "That's what reporters do. We go where the action is! Besides, I wanted to be anonymous so I could get a real scoop. And I have!"

The Aldens burst out laughing at their mistake. "Great, great," said the reporter. He turned to the photographer. "Did you get that shot, Mac?"

"You were great, Caryn," said Henry.

Caryn gave Henry an excited little hug and he blushed as shyly as Violet. "Sunny was great," she said, "thanks to you and your brother and sisters."

"And Watch!" said Benny. He let go of his end of the banner, and flung his arms around Caryn and then around Sunny. "Watch is the one who really solved the mystery. He proved it was Sunny at Dr. Scott's. Watch is a champion, too."

"He certainly is," said Caryn. She smiled down at Benny. "Hooray for Watch!"

"Hooray for Sunny and for Watch!" cried Benny.

# THE GUIDE DOG MYSTERY

### created by
## GERTRUDE CHANDLER WARNER

*Illustrated by Charles Tang*

ALBERT WHITMAN & Company
Morton Grove, Illinois

# Contents

Chapter        Page

1. A Special Kind of Dog    1
2. A Big Black Car    11
3. Someone Hiding in the Woods    23
4. Barking Dogs    34
5. The Mysterious Visitor Returns    43
6. A Crumpled Note    52
7. A Late Night for Benny    65
8. "Someone's Following Us!"    77
9. Ginger's Been Kidnapped!    88
10. Lots of Surprises    101

CHAPTER 1

# A Special Kind of Dog

"I wish we had a mystery to solve," Benny Alden said, kicking a stone that lay in the road. Benny was six years old and liked to do exciting things, like tracking down clues and finding suspects.

Benny's sister Jessie, who was twelve, was more patient. "I'm sure something mysterious will come along."

"Something always does," added their fourteen-year-old brother, Henry.

The Aldens had reached the grocery store

in downtown Greenfield. Their grandfather's housekeeper, Mrs. McGregor, had asked them to pick up some things for dinner. The others waited while ten-year-old Violet, wearing her favorite lavender sweater, tied their dog's leash to a parking meter. "We'll just be a minute, Watch," she told him. The dog lay down on the sidewalk.

"I wish Watch could come inside with us," said Benny. "He could help pick out his favorite dog food."

Watch's ears pricked up, and he quickly stood. But it wasn't the mention of dog food that had interested him.

"What is it, boy?" asked Henry.

Watch started barking loudly. The children looked in the direction Watch was facing and saw a young man with dark curly hair coming out of the grocery store. He was walking with a dog.

"I think Watch just spotted that golden retriever," said Violet.

"I thought Jessie said dogs weren't allowed in the grocery store," said Benny.

"From the dog's harness, I'd say that's a very special kind of dog," Jessie said, as the man and dog came closer. "It looks like a guide dog."

"What's that?" asked Benny.

"It's a dog that helps blind people," Jessie explained.

"If that man can't see, then why is he wearing a blindfold over his eyes?" asked Violet.

The children took a closer look. Violet was right. The man had a rolled-up scarf tied around his head, covering his eyes.

Watch was still barking, but Jessie managed to quiet him by gently stroking his head.

The man stopped on the sidewalk and the guide dog sat down beside him. The children watched as the man removed his blindfold and spoke to a red-haired woman who had been walking behind him.

"I'm going to go pat that dog!" cried Benny, running toward the golden retriever.

Benny squatted and reached out his hand toward the dog.

"You know, you really shouldn't distract a guide dog when it's working," the man told Benny, his voice gentle. "But it's okay this time."

"What do you mean?" Benny asked, as the other Aldens came to join him.

"I'm sorry if my brother is bothering you," Henry said to the man.

"Oh, no, it's quite all right. I enjoy meeting young people who are interested in animals," said the man with the curly hair. "I'm Jason Peters." He motioned to the woman beside him. "This is Mrs. Carter. She opened the Greenfield Guide Dog School just a few years ago. I work there as an instructor. And this is Ginger." He stroked the golden retriever's back. "She's one of my students."

"She looks like a very good student," said Violet, noticing how obediently Ginger sat at Jason's feet.

"As a matter of fact, she just passed her final exam," Jason said. "She was leading me, and Mrs. Carter was walking behind to make sure Ginger did everything right."

"Is that why you were wearing a blind-fold?" asked Jessie.

"Yes," Jason said. "I had to make sure Ginger would be able to lead someone who couldn't see. Now that she's completed her training, a blind person can use Ginger to get around. They'll be able to go to stores and restaurants, ride on buses, even cross busy streets, and never have to worry."

"That's amazing," said Henry. "How did you teach Ginger to do that?"

"It takes a lot of training," Jason explained. "If you'd like to come by the school tomorrow, I'll show you how we work."

"Wow!" cried Benny.

"We'd love to!" said Jessie. "By the way, we're the Aldens. I'm Jessie, and this is Henry, Violet, and Benny."

"My goodness," said Mrs. Carter. "Are you James Alden's grandchildren?"

"Yes, we are," answered Henry.

"I went to college with your grandfather. We've been friends for years," Mrs. Carter said. "I'd hoped to someday meet the wonderful grandchildren he's always talking about."

There was a whining sound behind them, and everyone turned to see Watch, still sitting by the parking meter. He was getting restless.

"That's *our* dog," said Benny proudly, as Jessie walked over and untied Watch's leash from the meter. She led him over to meet Jason, Mrs. Carter, and Ginger. After the two dogs had sniffed each other, Jessie told Watch to sit down, and he sat quietly at her feet.

"Do you think he could become a guide dog?" asked Benny.

"He might," said Jason, smiling at Benny. "He looks like a very good dog. But our school only uses special dogs that are trained from the time they're puppies."

"I can see that you children know how to handle animals," said Mrs. Carter. "I have an idea I'd like to discuss with your grandfather."

"What is it?" asked Benny eagerly.

Mrs. Carter just smiled. "I think I'll wait and speak with him first." She looked at her watch. "Oh! I've got to run. Nice meeting you all. See you later, Jason."

As Mrs. Carter hurried off, the children wondered what her idea was. They were so thrilled about visiting the guide dog school that they almost forgot to buy the things Mrs. McGregor had asked them to get for supper!

That evening, the children could hardly wait for their grandfather to get home so they could tell him about their plans for the next day. It was almost dinnertime. They sat in the old boxcar on the lawn behind their grandfather's house and listened for his car.

The boxcar hadn't always been in that spot. It used to be in the woods. When their parents had died, the children had run away and lived in the boxcar. But then their kind grandfather had found them and brought them to live with him. They'd been very happy ever since. The only thing they'd missed was their boxcar, and so Grandfather had moved it to the backyard.

"I think I hear Grandfather's car now!" cried Benny, jumping up and running out the door of the boxcar. The other children followed.

Sure enough, Grandfather was just pulling into the garage.

"Grandfather! Grandfather!" they all cried, running up to him and giving him big hugs.

"What a nice welcome!" Mr. Alden said.

"Guess what!" said Benny. "We're going to visit a guide dog school tomorrow!"

"Are your suitcases packed?" their grandfather asked.

"We're just going for the day," Violet said.

"That's not what I hear," said Grandfather.

"What do you mean?" asked Henry.

"I got a phone call from my old friend Betsy Carter today, and she wants you to spend the week there," Grandfather explained. "There are extra rooms on the dormitory floor, where you can stay."

The children were so surprised that at first they didn't know what to say. But Benny was rarely quiet. "A whole week?" he asked.

"Yes," Grandfather said. "Betsy only has a small staff, and it seems that most of them are away on vacation, so she needs some help. If you aren't interested, I could always call her back — "

"Of course we're interested!" Jessie exclaimed. "What a week we're going to have!"

Benny's eyes lit up. "And maybe we'll even find a mystery!"

The others laughed, but they didn't realize that Benny was right.

CHAPTER 2

# *A Big Black Car*

The following afternoon, Grandfather drove the children to the guide dog school. The Aldens looked out the window with interest as they headed up the school's long, winding driveway. A brick building sat at the top of the hill. On the beautiful green lawn in front, several people walked about with dogs.

Grandfather stopped the car in front of the main entrance and the children piled out eagerly.

"Welcome!" called Jason, who'd been watching for the Aldens. He took the suitcases from Violet and Benny's hands. "I'll take you up to your rooms."

"I have to get to work," Mr. Alden said, getting back in the car. "I'll pick you up in a week! Be on your best behavior for Mrs. Carter. She's going to look after you."

"We will, Grandfather. Good-bye!" the children called as he drove off.

Jason led the children across the wide, sunny lobby and into the elevator. He pressed the button for the fourth floor. The children noticed that along with the number, each button had small bumps on it.

"Those bumps say the number in braille," Jason explained. "Blind people feel the bumps to know which button to push." As they passed each floor, a bell rang. "If you want to know what floor you're on, you don't have to see the number. You can just count how many times the bell rings," Jason told them.

At the fourth floor, they got off the elevator and walked down a hall lined with doors, like a hotel.

"What are all these rooms for?" asked Jessie.

"Remember I told you that I teach dogs?" Jason replied. "Well, I also teach people. When someone gets a guide dog, they have to learn how to work with the dog. So they stay here for a few weeks while they're learning. We had a couple of extra rooms for you."

Jason brought them to two small but comfortable rooms, side by side. One was for Henry and Benny, the other for Violet and Jessie. Each room had two beds, dressers, desks, and chairs. They dropped off their suitcases, and then Jason continued their tour.

"This building is shaped like a U," he told them. "If you ever need me, my room is on this floor, on the other side of the U."

"You live here?" Violet asked.

"Yes," Jason explained, "because I'm responsible for the dogs day and night. It's easier to live on the campus."

The third floor held offices, including Mrs. Carter's. The dining room and lounge were on the second floor.

"But where are the dogs?" asked Benny.

"Don't worry, that's where we're headed right now!" Jason answered, as he led the children out the back door of the main lobby.

Behind the main building, surrounded by dense woods, was a smaller building with a fenced-in yard. The yard was filled with dogs: German shepherds, golden retrievers, and Labrador retrievers. Some of the dogs were sniffing about; others ran back and forth barking.

"The dogs get their exercise out here," Jason explained. "Inside there's a separate area for each dog, with the dog's food, water, and a place to sleep."

"All of these dogs are going to be guide dogs?" asked Benny.

"Most of them will," Jason said. "We start with very special puppies, who are raised by local families. In their first year, the puppies get used to being around people, traffic, and

things like that. They also learn to be obedient, to follow simple commands like 'sit'
and 'stay.' When they're a little over a year
old, the families bring them back to the
school to be trained."

"You mean they have to give the dogs
back?" asked Violet. "How sad! I know I
couldn't give Watch up."

"It is hard, but the families know the dogs
are being trained for important jobs," Jason
said.

Jason walked over to the gate. "How about
if I show you one of the dogs I'm working
with now?" He slipped into the yard, careful
not to let any of the dogs out. He took a
black Labrador by the collar and led him out
to greet the Aldens.

"This is Zach," Jason said. The children
sat down on the grass and stroked Zach's
sleek coat. The dog rolled about on the grass
playfully.

"The training takes a few months," Jason
continued. "Our instructors decide whether
the dogs are fit to be guide dogs. They have

to be friendly, smart, obedient, and hard-working. The ones that pass the final exam, as Ginger did yesterday, are then matched with people who want a guide dog."

"Are there some dogs that fail?" asked Violet.

"Yes. Some dogs are too shy or too aggressive, or just don't follow the commands. They're given away as pets," Jason said.

"Is Zach going to be a guide dog one day?" asked Benny.

"I hope so. How would you like to watch me train him?" suggested Jason.

"That would be great!" said Henry.

Jason went into the kennel. The children noticed that Zach sat up alertly when Jason returned carrying a leather harness. "He knows when he sees the harness that it's time to stop playing and start working," Jason explained.

"They take their jobs very seriously, don't they?" said Jessie.

"They have to," Jason said. "People depend on them."

Jason let the Aldens feel the harness before he strapped it onto Zach. The straps around the dog's body were soft and comfortable, but the handle was firm, with a metal frame inside. Jason explained that a regular leash would be too loose and wouldn't allow the person and the dog to work together as well.

After he'd strapped on the harness, Jason stood up. "Come," he called to Zach, his voice firm.

Zach moved to Jason's left side and stood next to his left leg, waiting for the next command.

"Forward!" Jason said. Zach began to walk forward as Jason followed. "Notice how he walks slightly ahead of me, to lead me," Jason pointed out. "Other trained dogs are usually taught to heel, or walk slightly behind. But guide dogs need to lead their owners."

"Watch walks ahead — but usually it's because he's chasing squirrels," said Benny, and they all laughed.

"Right," Jason said to Zach, and the dog

turned to the right. "Left," Jason said, and Zach turned left.

"What a good dog!" said Violet.

Then Jason dropped a leather glove on the grass as they were walking. He walked a few more steps and then stopped. "Fetch," he said, letting go of the harness. Zach ran back and picked up the glove in his mouth. Then he came back and stood waiting at Jason's left leg.

"Good boy," Jason said, taking the glove from Zach's mouth. "Fetching is an important skill, in case a person drops something when he's out with his dog," Jason told the children. Then he turned his attention back to Zach.

"Sit!" Jason said, and Zach sat right at his feet. Then Jason said "Down!" and the dog lay down on the grass.

Jason broke into a grin. He was obviously very pleased with Zach's performance. "Good boy," Jason murmured over and over in a warm, kind voice as he rubbed Zach's head and back. "We don't reward the dogs with biscuits when they do well," he explained. "We just give them lots of praise."

The Aldens watched as Jason worked with Zach again and again on the same commands. Almost every time, Zach behaved perfectly.

One time a bird hopped across their path. Zach began to bark and chase after the bird, until Jason scolded him. Immediately, Zach returned to his position next to Jason.

"We don't punish the dogs when they misbehave, we just speak to them in an angry tone of voice," Jason said. "Soon he'll learn not to get distracted when he's working."

When Jason decided that Zach had worked hard enough, he took off the harness and led the dog back into the yard with the others. When Jason came back out, he had another dog with him.

"Hey, Ginger!" cried Benny.

"I thought you might like to say hello to her," Jason said. "Let's take her harness off now, since she's not working."

"I'll help," offered Jessie, bending over.

Benny crouched down next to Ginger, petting her back.

Ginger lay down in the grass next to the Aldens. Jessie stroked her long, golden fur, and Ginger closed her eyes. Suddenly, her eyes opened and she lifted her head.

"Ginger!" they all heard a voice calling.

Ginger got up and raced down the hillside. The children watched as a big black car pulled up at the curb, and a tall well-dressed blond woman got out. "Ginger!" she called again, opening her arms as the dog raced toward her.

"Mrs. Davis!" Jason said angrily, walking briskly down the hill. When he reached the woman, Jason began speaking to her in low tones. While they couldn't hear what the two were saying, the children could see how angry Jason looked.

"I wonder what's going on," Jessie said.

"Jason seemed so nice and friendly, but now he looks like a different person," said Violet.

The children watched in surprise as Jason

grabbed Ginger's harness and began pulling her back up the hill. "Please stop this, Charlotte," Jason called to the woman. "I've told you it's just not a good idea! You did a great job with her, but she belongs here now!"

The chauffeur of the car, a young blond man, stared straight ahead.

Mrs. Davis stood silently. Finally she got back in her limousine. "Take me home, Glen," she said, and the car pulled away.

"Jason — " Benny called out as he approached.

"I'm sorry, but I have work to do now," Jason said, walking past the children. He still seemed angry.

"Can we do anything — " Jessie began.

"Go eat dinner or something," Jason said. "I'm busy." And with that he led Ginger into the kennel and shut the door.

"I wonder what that was all about," Henry whispered to Jessie.

"I don't know, but there's definitely something going on," Jessie replied.

# CHAPTER 3

# Someone Hiding in the Woods

Following Jason's suggestion, the Aldens headed to the dining room. It was a bright, pretty room, and the smells coming from the kitchen were delicious. Each table was covered with a clean white cloth and decorated with a small vase of flowers. Tonight was Taco Night, and several students and instructors were enjoying the food and lively music. The children noticed that there were also several guide dogs, each one sitting quietly under its owner's chair.

After dinner the children took a stroll around the beautiful wooded grounds and then went back to their rooms to get ready for bed.

"I hope all those dogs don't bark and wake us up the way Watch sometimes does," said Benny.

But the dogs didn't make a sound.

The next morning the Aldens ran into Jason on their way to breakfast. He was cheerful and friendly, and he seemed to have forgotten whatever had upset him the night before. After a hearty breakfast of eggs and bacon, toast, and milk, the children went outside and watched as Jason worked with Zach and some other dogs.

Around noon, the children ran into Mrs. Carter, who was walking with a girl just four years older than Henry. She was very pretty and had shiny black hair that hung almost to her waist. The girl had one hand on Mrs. Carter's arm, and in the other hand she held a suitcase.

"Hello!" Mrs. Carter greeted the Aldens. "This is Anna Chang, a student who's come to start working with a guide dog. I was just telling her about you. This is Henry, Jessie, Violet, and Benny."

Anna smiled and said hello as each Alden shook her hand.

"Would you please take Anna up to her room? It's right next to yours. Then maybe you could all have some lunch," Mrs. Carter suggested.

"Sure," said Benny. "I'm really hungry!"

"I bet I'm even hungrier!" Anna said, and everyone laughed. The Aldens knew they had found a friend.

Anna placed her hand on Henry's elbow so that he could guide her. Jessie took Anna's suitcase. Once they were in Anna's room, Anna asked how the room was laid out. Violet showed her where the bed, dresser, desk, and chair were. Anna paid close attention, placing a hand on each. She wanted to be sure she would be able to find everything later, on her own.

During lunch, Anna told the children how excited she was to be getting a guide dog. "I've been blind since I was born," Anna told them, "and I've never really felt independent. Whenever I want to go somewhere — to school or a store or a friend's house — I always have to ask someone to help me."

"I can't imagine not being able to just get on my bicycle and go wherever I want," said Benny between bites of his grilled cheese sandwich.

"It must be really hard," Violet agreed.

"I've seen blind people using canes," said Henry, taking a sip of his milk. "Have you tried that?"

"Yes, but it's hard to get around. A guide dog gives you complete freedom. I start college in the fall, and for the first time in my life I want to really be on my own." Anna smiled broadly as she thought about her future.

"Your dog will be your best friend," said Jessie.

"Yes," Anna said. But the children noticed her smile had faded a little.

"What's wrong?" asked Violet.

"Oh, it's nothing," Anna said. She picked up her ham sandwich and then put it back down on her plate. "It's just that . . . I've never had a pet before. I hope I'll know what to do."

"Don't worry," Jessie said. "I'm sure they'll teach you everything you need to know."

After lunch, the Aldens took Anna out to the kennel, where she'd been told to meet Jason.

"This is Anna Chang," Henry said when they spotted Jason.

"Nice to meet you," Jason said. "I'll be teaching you how to work with your dog."

While Jason and Anna were talking, Benny thought he heard a rustling noise in the woods behind them. He walked over to see what it was. He wondered if one of the dogs had gotten out of the yard.

Benny saw someone peering through the trees. The person was very tall and dressed in a dark suit. That's odd, Benny thought. Why would someone be walking around in the woods behind the kennels? He started to wave, but as he lifted his arm, the person ducked behind a tree, as if he or she didn't want to be seen.

"Benny!" called Henry.

"Henry, there's someone — " Benny began.

"Come on!" Jessie cried. "Anna's first lesson is starting."

Not wanting to miss anything, Benny forgot about the person in the woods and hurried over to the others.

Jason was showing Anna the dog harness that he'd shown the children the day before. She felt the leather and held it the way Jason showed her. Then Jason held the bottom of the harness and they practiced for quite a while, with Anna giving the commands he had taught her, and Jason leading her back and forth on the grass.

"Make sure your voice is firm," Jason reminded her. "The dog needs to know that you're the boss. Well, are you ready to meet your dog?"

Anna nodded, a nervous look on her face. "I guess so."

"I'll be right back," Jason said. He slipped into the exercise yard and came back out a moment later with a dog on a leash. It was Ginger!

"Here she is," he told Anna. "Her name is Ginger. She's a golden retriever with a reddish golden coat."

Anna reached out her hand and Ginger sniffed it. Then Anna cautiously put her hand on Ginger's soft back and slowly began stroking her. A warm smile spread across Anna's face.

"I think you two should have a little time by yourselves, to get to know each other," Jason said.

"We'll go stop by Mrs. Carter's office and see if she has any work for us," Jessie said.

As they turned to say good-bye to Anna, they saw her sitting on the grass, speaking softly to Ginger. It looked as if she and the dog were going to get along just fine.

"Am I glad you're here!" Mrs. Carter told the children when they entered her office. "My secretary is on vacation, and I have to run to a meeting." She quickly explained what she needed them to do: file papers, move stacks of folders, answer the phone. "I'll be back in about an hour," she said as she left.

The children set to work sorting the papers on Mrs. Carter's desk. When the phone rang, they took turns answering it and writing down the messages.

After a short while Benny noticed a shadow through the smoked glass of Mrs. Carter's door. He wondered who it was and why the person didn't just come in. Then he remembered the figure he'd seen in the woods. Could it be the same person?

At last, whoever it was knocked on the door.

"Come in," Henry called.

The door opened slowly, and a man walked in and looked around. He was wearing a dark suit with a flower on the lapel. His hair was neatly groomed and he had a little mustache. He seemed confused.

"Can we help you?" Jessie asked.

"Yes . . . uh . . . I'm looking for the director," he said at last.

"Mrs. Carter's not here right now. Can we give her a message?" Henry replied.

"That dog out on the lawn. I want to buy her," the man said.

"But — " Jessie began.

"She's a beautiful golden retriever. I simply must have her," he went on.

"I don't think she's for sale," Henry said, realizing the man must mean Ginger. "She's a guide dog."

"What do you mean she's not for sale?"

the man said. "That's ridiculous. Just tell me the price."

"I'm sorry, sir. You'll have to ask Mrs. Carter," Jessie said.

The man looked around the room at the children and drew in a deep breath. Then he turned on his heel and left, as abruptly as he'd come.

"That was strange!" Violet said when the door had shut behind the man.

"It certainly was!" Henry agreed.

"I wonder if he's the same person I saw in the woods," Benny said.

"What person in the woods?" Jessie asked.

Benny told the others what he'd seen earlier that day.

"There seem to be some strange things going on around here," Jessie said.

"Yes. Remember that scene between Jason and that woman — Mrs. Davis — yesterday?" Violet reminded them.

"I'm not sure about this," Henry said, "but I think we may have another mystery on our hands!"

# CHAPTER 4

# Barking Dogs

When Mrs. Carter returned, Henry told her about the strange man who'd wanted to buy Ginger.

"Well," she said, "sometimes people *do* want to buy the dogs."

As the Aldens got off the elevator on the second floor, they saw Anna on her way to the dining room. Benny ran to catch up with his new friend. Just before he reached her, she turned around and said, "Hello, Benny!"

Benny stopped in his tracks, his eyes wide.

"How did you know it was me?" he asked.

Anna smiled. "I just knew."

Benny didn't know what to say.

Anna laughed. "Besides," she said, "your shoes squeak when you run. I noticed that when I first met you."

"That's amazing!" Benny said as his sisters and brother joined him.

"Not really," Anna said. "Since I can't see, I have to be more aware of sounds and smells and other things," she explained. "I know Violet must have just come over, because I can smell her shampoo."

"Here I am," Violet said with a grin.

During a dinner of burgers and fries, Anna told them all about her afternoon and introduced them to a few of the other students she'd met that day. Anna and Ginger had gotten along very well, and the next day Jason was going to start their training together. She couldn't wait.

When they'd finished their strawberry shortcake, Anna and the Aldens went to the lounge to listen to music and talk.

At last, worn out from a busy day, the children went back to their rooms.

"I'm going to sleep well tonight!" Benny said.

But he was wrong.

A few hours later, Benny sat up in bed. He looked over at Henry, who was sleeping soundly. Benny wondered what had awakened him. In a moment he realized what it was. Outside his window the dogs were barking. They sounded upset.

Benny was just about to look out the window when he heard a soft tapping at the door. "Who is it?" he whispered.

"It's Jessie and me," he heard Violet whisper back.

Benny opened the door and the two girls hurried in.

"What's going on?" Henry asked, rubbing his eyes and sitting up.

"Something's disturbing the dogs," Jessie said.

"Or someone," said Violet, who was

standing by the window. "Come here, quick!"

The others hurried over and looked out.

"What is it?" Benny asked.

"I thought I saw someone looking in one of the kennel windows," Violet said. "But then the person disappeared."

The children all stood looking out the window as the dogs continued to bark. But all they could see was the dark kennel building.

"Maybe I imagined it," Violet said after a few moments.

The children kept watching for several more minutes, and then the dogs began to quiet down.

"If someone was there, they must be gone now," Jessie said.

"Who do you think it was?" Benny asked.

"I couldn't tell," Violet said. "Why would someone be lurking around in the middle of the night?"

"I don't know," Henry answered. "We'll ask Jason tomorrow. For now, I'm going to sleep."

\* \* \*

When they asked Jason the following day, he didn't seem to think that the barking dogs were anything to worry about. "I used to wake up every time they barked, but I don't anymore. Sometimes it's a rabbit or a skunk — it's not usually anything to worry about."

"What about the person Violet saw?" Jessie asked.

"It was probably just a shadow of a tree or something. I wouldn't worry about it," Jason advised.

Then Anna arrived for her first lesson with Ginger, and the Aldens forgot all about the barking dogs. Jason told them to watch from a bench in front of the school. They had to be quiet so they wouldn't distract Anna or Ginger.

Jason put Ginger's harness on her and placed Anna's hand on the handle. While the Aldens watched, the threesome began moving down the walkway.

"Give her lots of praise, and pat her head

when she does what you want her to do,"
Jason told Anna.

Anna was nervous, and at first she almost
tripped over Ginger as they walked. But soon
she was moving slowly down the sidewalk.
Jason stayed beside them, letting Anna and
Ginger lead the way.

"Uh-oh," Benny whispered when he saw
Anna and Ginger heading toward a large
rock on the path. But Ginger led Anna
around it.

As they approached the tree-lined driveway, a large branch hung overhead. "Oh, no!
Anna's going to bump her head," Violet
whispered. Ginger could easily have walked
under the branch, but she had been trained
to notice things that might get in the way of
the person she was leading. So she carefully
led Anna around the branch.

"That's amazing!" Jessie whispered.

At the curb, Ginger stopped and waited
for Anna's command. Jason explained, "Ginger will stop at the curb, while you listen for
traffic. If it's quiet, you can tell her to go

forward. But she'll only move forward if she thinks it's safe."

"You mean she'll disobey me?" Anna asked.

"Yes," Jason said. "Guide dogs are obedient, but they're also intelligent. If a situation is dangerous — for instance, if you tell them to step out into a street with cars going by — they'll disobey you. They've been trained to think of your safety first."

Anna bent and gave Ginger a big hug. "I know I'll be safe with Ginger," she said.

The children watched the rest of Anna's lesson with great interest. It was almost time for lunch when Benny whispered to the others, "Hey, look over there." He pointed toward the road in front of the school. A big black limousine was slowly driving by.

"Mrs. Davis again!" Jessie said.

The back windows of the car were tinted, so the children couldn't see inside. They could only see her driver, who was wearing dark sunglasses, in his uniform in the front seat.

"I wonder what she's up to!" Henry said.

"I hope she's not going to interrupt Anna's lesson. Jason would be upset," Violet said.

The children watched as the limousine started to turn in the driveway.

"Oh, no! Here she comes!" said Jessie.

But at the last minute, it seemed Mrs. Davis changed her mind. There was a skidding noise as the car came abruptly to a stop. The limousine swerved back into the street. Then the engine roared and the car pulled away quickly, sending up a cloud of dust and pebbles.

Jason looked up when he heard the noise. "What was that?"

"It looked like Mrs. Davis's limousine," Henry said.

A shadow seemed to pass over Jason's face. "I think we've done enough today," he said to Anna. "Why don't you and Ginger take a break?" And with that, Jason walked quickly away.

Once again, the Aldens were left wondering what was bothering him.

CHAPTER 5

# The Mysterious Visitor Returns

That afternoon, the Aldens
were sitting with Ginger on the school's front
lawn when a car pulled into the driveway
and stopped. A man got out, and the children
saw it was the same mysterious man who'd
tried to buy Ginger the day before.

"Ah, just who I was looking for," he said
as he walked toward the children. His voice
was smooth and friendly, but the Aldens
couldn't help thinking he sounded a little *too*
friendly. The man reached out to stroke Gin-

ger's back, and Henry stepped away, holding her leash firmly. "If you're still interested in buying Ginger, you'll have to speak to the director of the school, Mrs. Carter."

"I should have introduced myself yesterday," the man said. He smiled broadly, but his smile seemed false. "My name's Gerard Dominick, and I just happen to be the owner of some of the greatest champion dogs in the country." He paused, waiting for the children to make some response. When they said nothing, he continued. "This golden retriever would perfectly complete my collection of dogs. I can see that she's a champion. I'll make a generous offer — "

"We told you, you have to ask Mrs. Carter," Henry repeated.

"Come, come, now," Mr. Dominick said, taking his wallet out of his pocket. "This dog is worth a fortune! Who's going to know if you just hand her over to me? You can say she ran away."

"That's terrible!" Jessie said. "You'd better leave!"

"Hey, calm down," Mr. Dominick said nervously. He put his wallet back in his pocket. "All right, all right, I'm going. But I'm not giving up!"

The Aldens watched as Mr. Dominick got back in his car and drove off.

"I don't like that man at all," Violet said.

"Neither do I," Benny agreed.

"Do you think we should tell Mrs. Carter about him?" asked Jessie.

"She didn't seem too interested yesterday," said Henry.

"Maybe we should tell Jason," Violet suggested.

The children went straight to Jason's room on the fourth floor. They were about to knock on his door when they heard his voice inside.

"It sounds as if he's on the phone," Jessie said. "Maybe we should come back later."

While the children were deciding what to do, they couldn't help overhearing what Jason was saying on the telephone. "It makes me very uncomfortable. I just don't know if it's a good idea." He paused. "All right, if you think so . . . " Jason sighed. "Okay, I'll do it."

The Aldens heard Jason hang up the phone, and a moment later, his door opened. Jason stood in the doorway, very surprised to see the children. His face turned a deep shade of red. "What are you doing here?" he asked.

"We just wanted to, um — " Jessie began.

"There's something I have to take care of," Jason said abruptly. And before they could tell him about Mr. Dominick, he was gone.

"I know it isn't right to listen to other people's conversations," said Violet as the children headed back to their rooms, "but did anyone else hear what Jason was saying on the phone?"

"Yes," said Henry. "I wonder what he was talking about. What could be making him so uncomfortable?"

"It sounds as if he's going to do something he doesn't want to do," said Jessie.

"What could it be?" asked Benny.

"And who do you think he was talking to?" asked Violet.

"Maybe it was Mrs. Davis," said Henry. "Remember the other day he told her something wasn't a good idea? He used those same words on the phone just now."

"Whatever he was talking about, he didn't seem very happy to see us on his doorstep when he came out," Jessie pointed out.

"I noticed that, too," said Violet. "He was acting *guilty* about something."

The children all thought about that for a moment. At last Benny broke the silence. "This is getting more and more mysterious!"

That night, the children ate dinner with Anna before returning to their rooms and getting into bed. They quickly fell asleep. But once again, they were awakened at midnight by the sound of barking.

"Something's bothering the dogs again," Violet said, pushing back her blankets and getting out of bed.

"I wish they would be quiet," Jessie said groggily.

Just then there was an urgent knock at the door. "Open the door! Hurry!" Benny called.

Violet went to the door and opened it. "What is it?"

Benny and Henry ran past her to the window. "Look!" Benny said, pushing aside the curtains.

Jessie and Violet followed and looked at the building opposite theirs, where the boys were pointing. All the rooms were dark.

"What are we looking at?" Violet asked.

"It better be something good or I'm going back to bed," Jessie complained.

"There!" Benny cried. A light had just appeared in the window directly across from theirs. And just as suddenly, it was gone.

"That was strange," Violet said.

"It doesn't look like light from an ordinary lamp, does it?" Henry said.

"No, it doesn't," Jessie agreed.

"Look! There it is again!" Benny called. Now the strange light was shining from a different window.

"It's moving!" said Violet.

"Why would the light be moving?" Henry asked.

"There must be someone over there with a flashlight!" cried Jessie.

"Yes! You're right," Henry said.

"But why use a flashlight inside?" asked Benny. "Why not just turn on a lamp?"

The children watched as the light went off. After several minutes, they decided that whatever had been happening there was finished. Henry pulled the curtains closed, being careful not to knock Violet's paint set off the window ledge where she had left it.

"Maybe the lightbulb burned out and the person who lives in that room has to use a flashlight," Violet said.

"I guess that's possible," Jessie said. But none of them believed it for a minute.

"I think someone was looking for something in that room. Someone who wasn't supposed to be there," said Henry.

"And he didn't turn on the overhead light because he was afraid someone would see him," Jessie finished Henry's thought.

"But someone *did* see him," Benny said. "*We* did!"

"Now we just have to figure out who it was, and what he was looking for," said Violet.

Benny yawned loudly.

"There will be plenty of time for that tomorrow," said Henry.

# CHAPTER 6

# A Crumpled Note

The next morning after breakfast, the children went to the kennel to help Jason bathe the dogs. But they were surprised to find the building locked up tight. When they knocked on the door, there was no answer.

"Jason must not be here yet," Henry said.

The children sat down by the front door of the kennel to wait for him.

After several minutes, Jessie asked,

"Where do you think he is? He's usually here first thing in the morning."

"Maybe he's just running a little late," Benny said.

The children waited a few more minutes before Violet said, "I think something might be wrong."

"Let's go to his room and see if he's there," Henry suggested.

When the children got to Jason's room, he was just about to leave. He looked upset.

"Hi, Jason. Is everything okay?" Jessie asked.

"No, actually everything is *not* okay," he said angrily, letting the children into his room. "I've spent the whole morning looking for my key to the kennel and I can't find it anywhere. I was just on my way to Mrs. Carter's office to borrow hers."

"When was the last time you used your key?" Violet asked.

"Last night, around dinnertime. Then I left it in this box on my desk, like I always do." Jason lifted the top of the box so the children could see that it was empty.

"Maybe if we helped you look, we could find it," Henry suggested.

"I really need to get over there and feed the dogs," said Jason. "But if you want to stay here and look, that would be great."

"Are you sure you don't mind us going through your things?" Jessie asked.

"Not at all!" Jason said. "I've got nothing to hide."

Jessie recalled the conversation they'd overheard the day before and all the strange things that had been going on at the school, and she wondered if that was really true.

"Don't worry, we'll find it," said Violet as Jason left.

The children looked everywhere in Jason's room. Jessie looked under the bed. Violet searched the closet. Henry looked behind the chair and lamp. Benny searched the bookcase.

"Do you think it might have fallen in the wastebasket?" Benny asked, standing beside

a small basket with a few crumpled pieces of paper inside.

"Maybe," said Jessie.

Benny poked through the crumpled papers. "Hey, I think I've found something," he called out suddenly.

"The key?" asked Henry.

"No . . . but I think it's a clue," said Benny.

The others came over to see what Benny was holding. "I know you aren't supposed to read other people's letters, but this was in the trash and I couldn't help seeing what it says . . . "

"What is it, Benny?" Jessie asked.

Benny held out a crumpled piece of pink paper with the name *Charlotte Davis* printed at the top in gold letters.

Jessie took it and read the note aloud. "*Meet me tonight at eleven o'clock at Joe's Restaurant. It's important I speak to you. Please don't tell anyone.*"

"Is there a date on it?" Henry wanted to know.

"Yes. It was written yesterday," said Jessie.

"I wonder what was so important," Violet said.

"And why she didn't want him to tell anyone," said Benny.

"Do you think Jason and Mrs. Davis are plotting something?" asked Henry.

"It certainly does sound like it," Jessie said.

"Maybe that's who he was talking to yesterday on the phone," said Violet.

"We can talk about this later," Henry said. "For now, we'd better look for Jason's key."

The children resumed their search. They looked everywhere, but they didn't find the key.

"Well, I guess it's not here," said Jessie.

"We might as well go tell Jason," Henry said.

The children were taking one last look around the room when suddenly Violet ran to the window.

"What is it?" asked Benny.

"Look!" Violet said.

"All I see is the other wing of the building," said Jessie.

"That's just it!" Violet said, her voice excited. "That's the wing our rooms are in!"

"But what does that matter?" asked Jessie.

"That's our window right there!" Violet said, pointing. "See, there's my paint set on the windowsill!"

The others looked. Just as Violet said, in the window across the way they could see a paint box resting on the sill.

"That's neat! Our room is right across from Jason's!" Benny said.

"Don't you get it?" asked Violet. "Last night, when we saw the strange light, it was *here*! In this room!"

"You're right! We'd better get going, though," Henry said, "or Jason is going to wonder what's happened to us!"

The children hurried to the kennel, where Jason had already started washing the dogs.

A German shepherd stood in a large tub of water. Jason was rubbing the dog's black and tan fur with shampoo, making big soapy suds.

Jason looked up when the Aldens entered. "Did you find my key?" he asked hopefully.

"No, we didn't," Henry said.

"We looked everywhere," Jessie added.

Jason shook his head and sighed. "Thanks for trying. I can't imagine what could have happened to it. I guess I'll have a copy made from Mrs. Carter's."

"What can we do to help you with the dogs?" asked Violet.

"Cleo is ready to be rinsed," Jason said, handing Violet a hose. "Why don't you do it, and then Benny can towel her off. I hope you don't mind getting wet, Benny. Cleo usually shakes water all over me when I dry her."

"Great!" Benny said with a laugh.

Violet took the hose and began to spray the lather off of the German shepherd's back.

Cleo shook, and sprayed water all over a laughing Benny, who stood by with a fluffy white towel.

"Meanwhile, Jessie and Henry can help me get another dog started," Jason said.

Following Jason's instructions, Jessie got another large tub and began filling it with water. Henry went with Jason to get a brown dog with a smooth, glossy coat.

"What kind of dog is that?" asked Benny. "It doesn't have much fur."

"This is Ali," Jason said. "He's a boxer. Because boxers are short-haired, they can be used for people who are allergic to animals."

While Jessie and Henry washed Ali, Benny and Violet helped Jason wash another German shepherd.

Benny said as he reached for the bottle of shampoo, "What do you do at night, Jason? Do you go into town?"

Jessie gave Benny a sharp look. She knew what he was up to.

"Funny you should ask," Jason said. "Last night was unusual. I got a note from Charlotte Davis — you know, Ginger's former owner? She asked me to meet with her."

"And did you?" asked Benny.

"Benny!" Jessie scolded. "Don't be so nosy!"

A strange look passed over Jason's face. "I drove all the way to Joe's Restaurant and waited a long time, but she never showed up. It was after midnight by the time I got home."

"I wonder why she didn't show up," said Benny. But before he could say anything more, Jason changed the subject.

That night, when the Aldens sat down for dinner, Jessie turned to Benny. "I can't believe you asked Jason what he did at night!" she said.

"We wanted to find out if he'd met with Mrs. Davis, didn't we?" Benny asked.

"Yes, but . . . " Jessie began. She sighed and took a bite of her hamburger.

"But *what*?" Benny demanded.

"I think what Jessie's trying to say is that

you have to be a little more tactful," Henry explained, taking a sip of his milk.

"What does 'tactful' mean?" asked Benny.

"You have to be more careful of what you say to people, and not pry into their private lives," said Henry.

"Well, anyway, I wonder why Mrs. Davis didn't show up," Benny said. He dipped a french fry in ketchup and looked at it thoughtfully before popping it in his mouth.

"That *is* odd," said Jessie. "Especially since she said in her note that it was important."

"Remember what else Jason said? He said he didn't get home until after midnight. So he couldn't have been in his room when we saw those lights," said Violet.

"That's right! That means someone else was poking around here," Henry said. "I wonder what they were looking for."

"The key!" cried Jessie. She looked around and realized that several people at the other tables were looking over at her. "The kennel key," she said more quietly.

"But how did the person know that Jason

wouldn't be home?" asked Violet. Then her eyes lit up. "Unless — "

"Unless it was Mrs. Davis! Maybe she sent Jason that note just to get him out of his room!" Jessie said. "That would explain why she never showed up at the restaurant!"

The Aldens were all very excited about what they'd figured out. It was always fun trying to put together clues.

"But why would Mrs. Davis want the key to the kennel?" asked Violet.

"There is another possibility," said Henry. "Maybe Jason wasn't telling us the truth. He seemed very uncomfortable talking about last night, and he immediately changed the subject."

"Hey, there's Anna," said Benny. "Come join us!" he called to her.

Henry pulled over an extra chair so that Anna could sit down. Ginger lay down under Anna's chair. Violet asked how her day had been.

"It was fine," Anna said. "But I don't know . . . "

"Is something wrong?" asked Jessie.

"No — not with me," Anna said. "But during our afternoon lesson, Jason seemed to be acting strangely."

"What do you mean?" asked Henry.

"He just seemed kind of . . . nervous," Anna explained.

"I wonder why he'd be nervous," Violet said.

"Oh, never mind," said Anna. "I'm sure it's nothing."

The Aldens looked at one another. They were all thinking the same thing. Was Jason up to something?

# CHAPTER 7

# A Late Night for Benny

That night, the Aldens decided to keep watch out the window, to see if anything strange happened — like moving lights or fleeting shadows or barking dogs. They each agreed to take a two-hour shift while the others slept.

Benny had the first shift, from ten o'clock to midnight. While the others curled up in their beds, he sat by the window, looking out. At first it was fun staying up so late. He played cards and sipped a cup of juice and checked the window every few minutes.

But soon Benny began to feel sleepy. The room was dark, and the sound of Henry's slow, peaceful breathing made him want to crawl into his own bed. Looking out the window, he could see nothing out of the ordinary. All the windows across the way were dark. Benny knew everyone was probably asleep, just as he wished he were.

He looked at his watch. It was only eleven-thirty — he still had another half hour to go! His eyelids felt so heavy. He let out one long slow yawn, and then another. Each time he blinked, it was harder to open his eyes again.

Benny forced his eyes open wide and stared out the window, trying not to blink. But it was no use. Soon his eyes were closing again.

He didn't want to let the others down. What if something important happened and they missed it because Benny couldn't stay awake? He knew he had to do something or he would fall asleep.

Benny went into the bathroom. He turned

on the cold water and splashed some on his face. That helped a lot.

He went back to his seat by the window feeling better, but soon his eyelids were heavy again. He leaned his elbows on the windowsill and put his head in his hands. He wanted so much to put his head down — just for five minutes. What could be the harm? Benny crossed his arms on the windowsill and rested his head on top.

Suddenly he woke with a start. His arm had slipped off the sill. For a moment, he didn't know where he was. Then he remembered. He was supposed to be keeping watch. How long had he been asleep? he wondered.

Benny peered at the clock and saw that it was twelve o'clock. He smiled. It was time to wake up Henry, who was doing the next shift.

Before he woke Henry, Benny took one last peek out the window. There were no lights in the rooms across the way. He checked the kennel off to the left. And then he spotted something. From behind a tree, a shadow moved.

The shadow moved again, and this time Benny was sure he'd seen it. As if to prove this fact, the dogs began barking.

"Henry, Henry, wake up!" Benny called, his eyes glued to the window.

Henry stirred slowly. "Is it my shift already?" he asked.

"Yes, but I think I see something!"

Henry bolted out of bed and in a moment he was standing next to his brother. The two boys looked out the window.

"I saw a shadow by the kennel, and — " Benny began. "Look! There's a light moving around in the kennel! Someone's in there!"

Henry ran to get the girls while Benny kept watch.

When the girls joined them, they all agreed. It appeared that someone was snooping around in the kennel with a flashlight.

"If they're using a flashlight, I'm sure they're not supposed to be there," said Jessie.

"I bet it's the person who stole Jason's key!" cried Jessie.

"We'd better go tell somebody!" Benny said.

"Jason!" said Henry.

The children ran out of the room and all the way down the hall. They ran and ran, around two corners, to Jason's room.

"Jason! Jason! Wake up!" the Aldens called as they pounded on his door.

In a moment the door was opened by a very sleepy-looking Jason. "What is it?" he wanted to know.

"Come quickly! Someone's broken into the kennel!" Jessie said.

Jason looked confused. "What are you talking about?"

"Jason!" Henry said. "There's no time to explain. Come on!"

Jason sighed heavily. "You kids and your imaginations."

"It's not our imagination," Jessie said. "But if you don't believe us, we'll go by ourselves." The children started down the hallway.

"All right, I'm coming," Jason said, following them.

When they reached the kennel, they found the door was open, and the sound of barking dogs was deafening. As they peered into the dark building, they could see a flashlight shining down the hallway ahead of them.

Jason flicked on the overhead light, and the Aldens saw someone down the hall duck behind a large box. "Hello? Is there somebody there?" Jason called out. "Please come out at once!"

There was no response at first. Suddenly a figure darted out and began running down the hall away from them.

"He's heading for the back exit," said Jason. "I'll go around that way and try to head him off!"

The others ran down the hall after the figure. But before they could catch him, he'd run out the back exit. The heavy door slammed shut behind him.

The Aldens pushed open the door and looked out. There was a rustling in the woods. Jason stood next to the door, out of breath.

"Whoever it was, he took off into the woods before I could get to him," Jason said when he'd caught his breath.

"We'd better make sure the dogs are okay and that everything is in order," Jessie said.

The Aldens helped Jason go through the building and check each dog. Zach, Ginger, and the other dogs were all in their individual pens, just as they were supposed to be.

"Let's get back to bed," Jason said.

"Wait a minute," called Violet, who had gone back to take another peek at Ginger. "What are all these scratch marks on the gate to Ginger's pen?"

Jason came over to take a closer look. "That's odd," he said. "It looks as if someone was trying to break into her pen. There's a special latch on every pen so that the dogs can't get out. I guess the person who was in here was after Ginger." Jason twisted the

latch and opened the gate. Ginger came out and began sniffing at Jason. "Are you okay, girl?" Jason said, rubbing her back. When he was satisfied that she was unharmed, he led her back into her pen.

"What are we going to do? The person that sneaked in here probably used your key," Henry said. "He could come back."

"I'll camp out here tonight," said Jason, "and I'll talk to Mrs. Carter in the morning. We'll have to have the locks changed."

"Are you sure you'll be okay?" Violet asked.

"We'll bring you some blankets and a pillow," Jessie suggested.

"We could stay with you," Benny offered.

"No sense in all of us staying up," Jason said.

After making sure that Jason was settled for the night, the Aldens returned to their rooms.

"It's a good thing you were on watch, Benny," Jessie told her brother.

"I can't believe you were able to stay awake so late," Violet said.

"Aw, it was easy," Benny said, hiding a smile.

"I shouldn't tell you this, but we all thought you'd fall asleep for sure," Jessie said.

Benny gave her a look. "What? I can't believe you'd think that."

Violet noticed that Henry had been walking along quietly beside them. "Thinking about something, Henry?" she asked.

"What?" Henry had been deep in his own thoughts. "Oh, well . . . I was just wondering . . . did anyone else think that Jason acted strangely tonight?"

"Not really," Jessie answered. "What do you mean?"

They had reached their rooms. Jessie opened the door to the girls' room and they all went inside and sat down on the beds to talk for a moment.

"Remember when we first told him someone had broken into the kennel?" Henry asked. "He kept saying he didn't believe us, before he finally came along. I wonder if he was stalling."

"Why would he do that?" Violet asked.

"Maybe he *knew* someone was going to break into the kennel," Henry said slowly. "Maybe he wanted to make sure we didn't get there before they finished whatever it was they were up to."

"Then why did he come with us after all?" Jessie asked.

"He knew we were going, so he had to come," Henry said. "Then when we got there, remember he went around the outside to head off the person inside? He said he couldn't catch the person — but maybe he wasn't even trying."

"But he seemed so out of breath," Violet said.

"That's just it," Henry said. "I wonder if it was all an act."

"Do you think that's why he offered to keep guard?" Jessie asked.

"And he didn't want us to stay with him. . . ." Benny said.

"I can't believe Jason is up to anything bad," Violet said.

Jessie sighed. "It's possible. But we really haven't got any proof.

"Tomorrow we'll have to do more detective work."

# CHAPTER 8

# "Someone's Following Us!"

The next day was bright and sunny, and while eating a breakfast of fresh orange juice and waffles they saw Jason in the dining room, huddled over a cup of coffee.

"Did anything else happen last night?" Benny asked.

Jason assured them that the rest of the night had been quiet.

"It's a beautiful day out," Violet noted,

looking out one of the large dining room windows.

"Perfect for Anna's first trip downtown with Ginger," Jason said. "Let's meet in the lobby in fifteen minutes. After we walk around downtown, we'll visit Greenfield College, where Anna will be going to school in the fall. Ginger needs to get used to being on the campus with all the students."

"We've driven past the college with Grandfather," said Violet. "It's very pretty."

"I have an idea," said Henry. "Maybe we could picnic on that big green lawn."

"That sounds great!" Jason said.

"We can pick up some food while we're downtown," Benny suggested.

"I'll go to the kitchen and see if we can borrow the other things we'll need," Jessie said. She was back in a moment with a red and white checkered tablecloth, some napkins, and a knife for cutting bread and cheese and fruit.

A short while later, the group was heading downtown. The children walked a slight distance behind so they wouldn't disturb Anna and Ginger's lesson.

Jason had prepared Anna for the trip by showing her a special map of town. The streets were marked with raised lines so that she could feel where they were. He had also asked her which stores she usually visited, so that she and Ginger could practice going in those.

"We're on Main Street now," Jason told her. "Let's walk to the pet shop on the corner of Spruce and Elm. That's a place you and Ginger will be going to often."

"That's where we buy things for Watch!" said Benny.

They all began walking. When they reached the first corner, Ginger stopped right at the curb.

"Good girl," Anna said.

"Listen for the traffic," Jason told Anna.

A couple of cars went by.

"It sounds quiet now," Anna said.

"Then tell Ginger to move ahead," Jason said.

"Forward," Anna said, and they all crossed the street.

At each corner Ginger would stop and wait for Anna to listen for the traffic and decide which way she wanted to go.

When they reached the pet shop, Jason showed Anna how to enter the store with Ginger.

As the Aldens paused outside, Benny moved closer to his sisters and brother and whispered, "I think someone's following us."

"You do?" Jessie asked. She looked behind them. The only person she saw nearby was a tall figure in a long raincoat and hat. The person was standing at a pay phone making a call. Jessie couldn't tell if it was a man or a woman. "Do you mean that person on the phone?"

"That's the one," Benny said. "I noticed him as soon as we got into town, and he's been with us this whole way."

"Are you sure?" Henry asked.

"Yes," said Benny.

"Now that you mention it, there is some-

thing odd about him," Violet said. "Why is he wearing a raincoat and hat on this beautiful, sunny day?"

"Look at the way he's standing," Jessie pointed out. "Head down, hat pulled low, back toward us — as if he doesn't want to be seen."

"Or recognized," Henry added.

"Who do you think it might be?" asked Violet.

"I don't know," said Benny. "Maybe Mr. Dominick. He's tall and thin."

"So is Mrs. Davis," said Jessie. "It could be a woman, you know. You really can't tell."

"We'll keep an eye on him — or her," said Henry.

A few minutes later, Anna, Jason, and Ginger came out of the shop. Anna was carrying a small paper bag. "Look what I got," she told the Aldens.

They crowded around as she pulled something out of the paper bag. It was a new collar for Ginger, made of soft brown leather.

"She's been wearing the same collar since she was a puppy," Jason said.

"The leather is all lumpy and cracked," Anna added.

"I think she'll really like the new one," Violet said.

"I'll put it on her tonight when we get home," Anna said, as she and the others began walking.

When they'd gone a few blocks, Jessie took a quick peek over her shoulder. The mysterious person was close behind them. Each time one of the Aldens looked back, the person would duck into a doorway or pause on a corner. But he — or she — never gave up.

The next stop was the grocery store. The Aldens followed Jason, Anna, and Ginger inside.

"Let's get some things for our picnic," Jessie said, picking up a basket.

First Ginger led Anna up the produce aisle. Just like outside, Ginger was a good guide. She carefully led Anna around a display of watermelons in the center of the aisle.

Henry picked out some ripe peaches and plums and put them in Jessie's basket. Violet selected a juicy tomato. Benny got a plastic bag and filled it with dried pineapple, raisins, and nuts, which he scooped from a large bin.

Next they came to the dairy case, where Violet picked out a piece of sharp cheddar and some Swiss cheese.

When they reached the dog food aisle, Ginger began to sniff at some of the bags of dried food on the shelves. "Ginger!" Jason scolded. Ginger quickly returned to the center of the aisle. "Good girl," Jason said.

Along the back wall was a bakery, where Jessie chose a long loaf of crusty bread. Benny picked out a carton of fruit punch.

"Now all we need are paper plates and cups," said Violet as she took some off of a shelf and put them in Jessie's basket. At last their picnic was complete.

As they were standing in line at the checkout counter, Henry noticed someone moving up the aisle behind Anna and Ginger. It was the same mysterious person who'd been following them. For the first time, Henry also noticed that the person walked with a limp. "Jessie!" Henry whispered. "There he — or she — is again! I'm going after him."

Henry set off to try to get a closer look. The person was following Anna and Ginger up the soap aisle when Henry called out, "Hey, you! In the raincoat!" The person quickly darted down the canned vegetable aisle, with Henry in pursuit, but he was able to outrun Henry. As Henry raced to the end of the aisle, the person ran out the front door.

Breathless, Henry returned to his sisters and brother, who had paid for their groceries.

"Well?" Jessie asked. "Could you see who it was?"

"No," Henry said, catching his breath. "He — or she — was too fast for me."

In a few minutes, Jason, Anna, and Ginger joined them at the front of the store. "What was going on back there, Henry?" Jason asked. "Why did you run past us?"

Henry was about to answer when Anna

interrupted. "Were you after that person who was following us?" she asked.

"Yes — you knew someone was following you?" Henry asked.

"I had heard footsteps behind me for several minutes. At first I thought it was just a coincidence, but it was always the same person," Anna said.

"How do you know?" Violet asked.

"I recognized the way he walked — with a slight limp," Anna explained. "He stopped and started whenever I did."

"Did you see who it was?" Jason asked Henry.

"No, he ran away too fast." Henry looked disappointed.

"So you don't know if it was the same person who was in the kennel last night?" Jason asked.

"No," said Henry. "Could you tell if it was him, Benny?"

"No," said Benny. "I couldn't see him."

"Wait a minute. What are you talking about?" Anna wanted to know. No one had told her what had happened the night before. They didn't want to upset her.

"Well?" Anna demanded.

"We'll tell you about it over lunch," Jessie said.

CHAPTER 9

# *Ginger's Been Kidnapped!*

Greenfield College was only a few blocks from downtown. Anna, Ginger, and Jason led the way, with the Aldens following. Jessie and Henry each carried a bag of groceries.

When they reached the college, they saw several big stone buildings, covered in ivy, around a large green lawn. Students carrying books and notebooks walked from one building to another. Some students sat on the grass eating lunch and chatting. On one side of the lawn, a couple of people were throwing a football.

Henry spotted a shady corner surrounded on two sides by tall bushes. "How about if we sit over there?" The others nodded and followed him across the lawn, being careful not to get in the way of the ball players.

Jessie got out the checkered tablecloth and spread it on the grass. Everyone sat down, and Ginger lay on the grass next to Anna. Violet placed a paper plate and cup in front of each person, and Benny handed everyone a napkin.

"What's for lunch?" Jason asked as Henry began to reach into one of the bags.

"Bread and cheese and fruit," Henry said. He placed all the food in the center of the tablecloth where everyone could reach. Jason tore off a hunk of bread and handed the loaf to Anna, who did the same.

Jessie cut the cheese into chunks and sliced the tomato with the knife she'd borrowed from the school's kitchen. Violet filled all the cups with punch.

For a moment everyone was silent, eating sandwiches of the bread and cheese and tomato. They scooped up handfuls of the dried fruit and nuts. At last, as they sat back enjoying the juicy peaches and plums, Anna asked the question that had been on all their minds. "Now, who was in the kennel last night?"

"That's just it — we don't know," Henry said. "Someone broke in — Benny spotted the person from our window. We went and woke up Jason, and then we all ran down to the kennel."

Jason picked up the story. "But when we got there, whoever was inside ran into the woods."

"What time did all this happen?" Anna asked.

"Around midnight," said Violet.

"What were you doing looking out the window at midnight, Benny?" Anna wanted to know.

"I was keeping watch. It was my shift," Benny explained.

"What do you mean, you were 'keeping watch'?" asked Jason.

The Aldens looked at one another. They hadn't really planned on telling anyone about all the strange things that had been happening at the school — at least not until they had some answers. They weren't even sure they could trust Jason. He might be involved somehow.

"Why were you keeping watch?" Anna said.

Benny looked to Jessie for help.

"Well," Jessie began slowly, "ever since we came to the school, we've noticed some strange things have been happening. The very first day Benny saw someone lurking in the bushes behind the kennel."

"Then there was this man, Mr. Dominick, who kept coming by trying to buy Ginger," Violet continued.

"*My* Ginger?" Anna put her arms around Ginger possessively. Jessie smiled, thinking how close Anna and the dog had become.

"The school doesn't sell dogs," said Jason.

"We told him we didn't think the school sold their guide dogs, but he wouldn't give up," Violet said.

"I still don't understand why you were keeping watch," Anna said.

"Does it have to do with that night you thought you saw someone lurking around the kennel?" Jason asked.

"Yes," said Benny. "And the night before last we saw some weird lights."

"Weird lights?" Jason repeated. "Where?"

"They were, um . . . " Benny paused, not sure what to say.

"Actually, Jason, they were in your room," Henry finished for his little brother. "We think someone was in there with a flashlight. And the next day, your key to the kennel was gone."

Jason sat back on the blanket, trying to take in what the Aldens had just told him. "This gets stranger all the time," he said at last. "Why would someone want to break into the kennel? Do they want one of the dogs?"

"Well," Anna said, "they're worth more than gold to people like me." She stroked Ginger's back.

"That reminds me," said Henry. "The latch on Ginger's pen was all scratched up last night. Remember?"

"And Mr. Dominick said something about Ginger being worth a lot of money — that she looked like a champion dog," added Jessie.

Anna sat up straight. "Do you think someone — Mr. Dominick — is trying to steal Ginger?"

"Could be," said Henry.

"I'm not going to let that happen," Anna said fiercely. "I'd feel safer if Ginger slept in my room tonight."

"That's usually not allowed at this point —" Jason began.

"I think it's a great idea," said Jessie, and the others nodded and looked at Jason expectantly.

"All right, but only because this is a special situation," Jason said.

After they were done eating, the children gathered up the garbage and threw it in a nearby trash can. Anna and Jason folded the tablecloth. Then they spent the rest of the sunny afternoon playing in the grass with Ginger. They were having so much fun that none of them noticed the tall person in the raincoat slinking away through the bushes.

After dinner, Anna brought Ginger back to her room instead of to the kennel. Each of the Aldens gave Ginger a pat on the head as they said good night.

"Her new collar is very nice," Violet said.

"I hope Ginger likes it, too!" Anna said with a smile. "Good night!"

The nights before had been very exciting. For a change, the Aldens were hoping they could get a good night's sleep.

But once again, something woke them. This time it was someone banging on the door.

"Jessie! Violet!" a voice called. "Wake up!"

Violet jumped out of bed and ran to the

door when she recognized Anna's voice. "Anna, what is it?" Violet asked.

"It's Ginger! She's been kidnapped!" Anna cried.

"What do you mean?" demanded Jessie.

"Someone broke into my room and took her!" Anna said.

Henry and Benny had just stumbled sleepily out of their room to find out what was going on. As soon as they heard what Anna was saying, Henry took off down the hall. "I'm going to get Jason," he called over his shoulder.

When Henry returned with Jason, Anna was sitting on her bed, wiping tears from her eyes. Jessie had gotten her a glass of water and Violet was sitting beside her, patting her hand. Benny was pacing restlessly back and forth.

"Tell us exactly what happened," Jason said.

"I was in bed," Anna began. "Ginger was sleeping on the floor next to the chair. I heard a scraping noise at my door — now I realize it must have been someone picking the lock. I heard the door open, and someone called Ginger's name. I thought I was dreaming. But when I heard the door click shut, I knew it wasn't a dream. Ginger was gone!"

"Then what did you do?" asked Jason.

"I ran out into the hallway and banged on Jessie and Violet's door," Anna said.

"When you opened the door, did you see anyone in the hallway?" Jason asked the girls.

"No. There was no one but Anna," Violet said.

"I know who the person was," Anna said.

"You do?" Jessie said.

"Oh, I don't know the person's name, but I know it was the same person who was following us today," Anna said.

"How can you be sure?" Henry asked. He noticed Ginger's old collar lying on Anna's desk and picked it up.

"I heard the way he ran. It was the same limp I'd heard earlier today, behind me," Anna said. "I also noticed that he smelled flowery — like aftershave or perfume."

"The person must have overheard us saying that Ginger was going to spend the night in your room," Violet said.

"I can't believe Ginger would just go off with a stranger," Jessie pointed out.

"Maybe it wasn't a stranger," said Benny. "Maybe it was Mrs. Davis."

Everyone looked at Benny. He could be right. The children all remembered the way Ginger had run eagerly to her former owner only a few days before.

As they were talking, Henry had been idly playing with Ginger's old collar. It seemed awfully lumpy. He noticed a small slit in the leather and slipped his finger in. All of a sudden, Henry called out, "Oh, my gosh! Look at this! There's something inside Ginger's collar!"

Everyone stopped talking and looked over. "What is it, Henry?" Jason asked.

Henry was pulling something out from inside the two layers of leather. It looked sparkly. At last he got the object out and held it up in the light where it glittered.

"It's a diamond bracelet!" Jessie cried. Everyone crowded around Henry to examine the valuable piece of jewelry.

"What was this doing inside Ginger's collar?" asked Anna, as she fingered the narrow bracelet.

"Why would someone tuck a diamond bracelet inside a dog's collar?" asked Violet.

"Oh, my goodness!" Jessie cried out. "Maybe the person who kidnapped Ginger wasn't after *Ginger* at all. Maybe the person knew the bracelet was in Ginger's collar, and that's what he was after!"

"You may be right," said Jason. "I think I'd better make a few phone calls." He picked up the phone, dialed, and began speaking quietly.

While Jason talked, the Aldens comforted Anna, who was quite upset.

"Don't worry, we'll solve this mystery and get Ginger back," Violet assured her.

"You don't know us very well yet, but we're good at solving mysteries," Benny added.

When Jason had hung up the phone, Henry asked if he'd spoken with the police. "No," Jason said. "I called Mrs. Carter. She wants to wait until tomorrow before we call the police. She's hoping we can figure out what happened to Ginger and where this bracelet came from. If we call in the police, it will be terrible publicity for the school, and we don't want that." The others all nodded.

"I called Charlotte, too," Jason went on. "She seemed very upset when I told her what happened to Ginger."

"Do you believe her?" Henry asked.

Jason looked thoughtful. "I guess so. She's going to come by tomorrow morning, and we can talk to her some more and show her the bracelet."

"Until then, I guess there's nothing more we can do," Jessie said.

CHAPTER 10

## Lots of Surprises

The following morning, the Aldens woke and dressed quietly. They were all wondering what had happened to Ginger and feeling very sorry for Anna.

"I have an idea," said Violet. "Let's get some flowers for Anna. They won't take Ginger's place, but they might make her feel a little better."

"The flower shop downtown is open early," said Jessie. "We could go right now."

In no time the Aldens were walking down

Main Street toward the flower shop. Suddenly, up ahead, they saw a tall person walking a golden retriever!

It was Mr. Dominick!

"Hey, you!" Benny cried out, breaking into a run. "Stop!"

The others chased after Benny, expecting Mr. Dominick to run away. But surprisingly, he came toward them.

"Well, hello," he called out, a broad grin on his face.

"You kidnapped Ginger!" Benny shouted angrily.

But as he got closer, Benny stopped in his tracks. The others stopped right behind him. The dog wasn't Ginger! It was a different golden retriever!

"Meet Lola," Mr. Dominick said. "When I realized I couldn't get Ginger, I searched all over and found a breeder who sold me this beautiful dog. I told you I wouldn't give up."

"But we thought you meant —" Jessie began.

"You thought I meant what?" asked Mr. Dominick.

"Oh, nothing," Jessie said, patting Lola on the head. "She is a beautiful dog."

"Her first show is in two months. Come see her win," Mr. Dominick said. "Bye-bye!"

The Aldens watched as Mr. Dominick and Lola walked off down the street. "Well, I guess Mr. Dominick wasn't the one trying to take Ginger," said Violet.

"Who could it be?" wondered Jessie.

Then they turned slowly and went into the flower shop. There they selected a pretty bunch of nice-smelling flowers that they thought Anna would like, and headed back to the school.

As the Aldens were walking up the school's driveway, they saw Jason walking just ahead of them. "Hey, wait for us!" Henry called out.

When Jason turned, the children noticed he had a strange look on his face. He was carrying something in a bag, which he quickly tucked behind his back.

"So you had some things to do this morning, too," said Jessie.

"Uh, yes," Jason said. He sounded uncomfortable.

"What's in the bag?" asked Benny.

"Nothing. . . ." Jason said. He seemed relieved when a car pulled into the driveway, interrupting their conversation. It was Charlotte Davis.

A few moments later they were all gathered in Mrs. Carter's office, along with Anna and Mrs. Carter. Jason showed the diamond bracelet to Mrs. Davis. "This was tucked inside Ginger's collar. Do you recognize it?"

"I think so," she said, taking the delicate piece of jewelry from him. "It looks like the heirloom bracelet that I haven't been able to find for a few months. I'll put on my glasses and then I'll know for sure." Mrs. Davis began patting her pockets, feeling for her glasses. "Now where did I put them?" she mumbled to herself. "Oh, I must have left them in the car."

"Can I run down and get them?" Henry offered.

"Thanks, but I'll just call down to my driver to bring them up." Mrs. Davis went to the window and called down to her car, which was parked just below. "Glen! Would you please bring my glasses? I think they're in the backseat."

A few minutes later, a tall man entered the room carrying an eyeglass case. As he crossed the floor to where Mrs. Davis was sitting, Benny gasped.

"What is it, Benny?" Jessie asked.

"It's him!" Benny said. "He's the one who was following us! I can tell by the way he walks."

Glen was walking with a limp. He stopped in the middle of the room and looked at Benny.

"Are you sure?" Jason asked.

"*I'm* sure," said Anna. Everyone turned to look at Anna, who'd been sitting quietly in the corner. "I recognize the sound of his walk

from the grocery store yesterday. And I can smell his aftershave — it's the same as last night."

Glen looked around nervously.

"You think Glen is the one who kidnapped Ginger?" asked Mrs. Davis.

"Why would I —" Glen said.

Just then, the door was pushed open and someone else came into the room. It was Ginger! Trailing from her collar was a broken piece of rope. Ginger ran around the room excitedly, her tail wagging wildly. Then she raced over to Anna.

In all the commotion, Glen forgot that the others were there. "Ginger! How did you get free?" he said, not realizing the others were listening.

"So it *was* you," said Mrs. Davis.

Glen realized it was over. He hung his head sadly and said, "Yes, I admit it, Mrs. Davis. I kidnapped Ginger and tied her up in my sister's backyard. It's just down the street from here."

"But why?" asked Violet. "Why would you do such a thing?"

"It was because of the bracelet, wasn't it?" said Henry.

"Yes," Glen said. He began speaking slowly. "I thought if I stole that bracelet I'd have all the money I'd ever need. I used to take Ginger for walks every day. So one day, when we were leaving, I sneaked into Mrs. Davis's room and took the bracelet."

"How did it end up in Ginger's collar?" Jessie asked.

"After I'd taken it, I saw Mrs. Davis coming. I panicked. I didn't want her to catch me with the bracelet! So I made a slit in Ginger's collar and hid it there." He sighed. "But I didn't know that the next day Ginger was being returned to the school for training."

"So all this time you've been following us and sneaking around, trying to get the bracelet back," said Jessie.

"Yes," Glen said.

"And you stole Jason's key and broke into the kennel," said Henry.

Glen nodded. "I wrote Jason a note and signed Mrs. Davis's name. I knew that he'd go meet with her and that would give me time to break into his room and find the key."

"So that's why you never showed up that night," Jason said to Mrs. Davis. "I knew you were upset about having to return Ginger. Oh, Charlotte. I thought you were going to ask for her back. I was going to tell you I couldn't do that."

"You kept telling me not to come back and see her again, but I missed her," Mrs. Davis said.

"She needed to become attached to Anna, and she couldn't do that if you kept coming back," Jason explained. "I was afraid that you were the one who'd been following us."

"And the one who kidnapped her?" Mrs. Davis smiled. "I would never have gone that far."

While they were talking, Mrs. Carter had

gone to the phone and quietly made a call. In a few minutes, the police appeared in the doorway.

"Jason, why don't you take Anna and the Aldens outside," Mrs. Carter suggested. "We'll handle this from here."

As they left Mrs. Carter's office, Jessie turned to the others. "At last the mystery is solved!"

"It's great that we can go for a walk now and not worry someone's following us," Violet added.

"I don't know about you guys, but solving a mystery always makes me hungry," said Benny.

"Oh, Benny," said Henry. "Everything makes you hungry."

"Well, I'm hungry, too," said Anna.

"How about a special celebration at the pancake house downtown," Jason suggested.

"Good idea!" Violet said.

A short while later, Jason, Anna, and the Aldens were all sitting around a big table enjoying stacks of delicious blueberry pancakes. Ginger sat happily under Anna's chair.

"There is still one thing I'm wondering about," Benny said. "What's in that bag you've been carrying around since this morning, Jason?"

Jason's face flushed. "Well, I might as well get this over with." He reached into the bag and pulled out a single red rose. "This is for you, Anna. I wasn't sure if this was a good idea, but . . . oh, what the heck. I'm hoping that maybe when we're done with your training . . . um . . . you and I could go out, you know, on a date."

Anna broke into a smile. "I'd like that very much."

Violet grinned. "So that's what was making you so nervous!"

"And that's what we overheard that day on the phone," Henry said.

"I was afraid you might have heard me when I came out of my room that day and saw you on my doorstep! That's why I took off so quickly. I was embarrassed," Jason said. "I'd been talking to my brother about Anna. I was afraid to ask her out, but he said I should."

"I'm glad you did," Anna said, taking his hand.

At last all the mysteries had been solved.

A few weeks later, Henry, Jessie, Violet, and Benny were in the pet shop in Greenfield when they saw a tall woman standing at the counter. Beside her was a golden retriever.

"Mrs. Davis?" said Jessie.

"Hello!" Mrs. Davis said. "This is Max. I had such a wonderful experience with Ginger that I decided to train another puppy for the school."

Just then Max began yipping excitedly. The Aldens turned to see that Anna had just entered the shop with Ginger. They moved smoothly together, like a team.

"Anna!" cried Benny.

"Hello, Benny," said Anna, walking over with a big smile on her face.

"Are you done with your training?" asked Henry.

"Yes. Ginger and I go everywhere together now. It's wonderful! My whole life has changed," said Anna. "She's even coming with Jason and me to a concert tonight."

Anna knelt down and Ginger turned and licked her face eagerly. Anna laughed out loud.

"It's good to know that everyone's happy," Violet said, stroking Ginger's back.

"Especially Ginger," said Benny. "She's a very special dog."

# THE MYSTERY OF THE MIDNIGHT DOG

### created by
## GERTRUDE CHANDLER WARNER

*Illustrated by Hodges Soileau*

ALBERT WHITMAN & Company
Morton Grove, Illinois

Printed in the U.S.A.

# Contents

CHAPTER                                               PAGE

1. Kudzu and Ghost Finders                             1
2. The Ghost Dog of Elbow Bend                        11
3. Howls in the Night                                 22
4. Clues in the Park                                  35
5. Tourists Keep Out?                                 49
6. No Footprints                                      65
7. An Exciting Discovery                              81
8. Setting a Trap                                     90
9. Whose Ghost Dog?                                  100
10. The Ghost Catchers Explain                       107

# CHAPTER 1

# *Kudzu and Ghost Finders*

"Look! It looks just like a dinosaur!" Six-year-old Benny Alden pointed out the window of the car.

Henry, Jessie, and Violet Alden looked where their younger brother was pointing, and Watch, their dog, sat up and put his paws on the edge of the window. Only Grandfather Alden didn't look, because he was driving.

"You're right, Benny," said Henry, who was fourteen. "It does look like a dinosaur."

"I *think* it's an old house that's falling

down," said Violet, who was ten.

"Or being mashed by all those green vines that are covering it," Jessie said, who was twelve and often acted motherly toward her younger sister and brother.

"Those green vines are everywhere!" Benny exclaimed. "What are they?"

"The vines are called kudzu," Grandfather Alden told him. "It's considered a weed in the South. People have to fight to keep it from covering everything. I've read it can grow up to four inches a day."

"A monster vine that eats everything," said Jessie.

Benny shivered and pretended to be afraid. He leaned over and said, "Watch, be careful! You don't want to get eaten by the monster vines!"

Watch, a small dog who acted as if he were much bigger, peered out the window and cocked his head. He wasn't sure what Benny was talking about, but he was ready to face it.

Henry, who was sitting in the front seat next to Grandfather, looked up from the map he held. "It looks like we're almost there," he announced. "According to the map, we're only about twelve miles from Elbow Bend, Alabama."

"We are?" Benny asked. "Good. I'm hot. And thirsty!" he said.

"Not hungry, too?" Henry teased Benny.

Benny thought about that for a moment. "Maybe," he said. "I could be hungry, too."

"Don't worry, Benny," Grandfather Alden said. "I'm sure Sally Wade will have a nice cold drink and something waiting for us to eat." Mrs. Sally Wade was an old friend of Grandfather's who had invited the Aldens to visit.

"Oh, good." Benny bounced a little on the seat with excitement. "Then the only other thing we'll need is a good mystery to solve. Let's ask Mrs. Wade if she has a mystery for us when we get there."

"We'll do that," Grandfather agreed. "Although it's a small town, Elbow Bend is famous for its fine old houses. It was one of the first settlements in the state. It's bound to have at least one haunted house."

"Not Mrs. Wade's house?" Benny asked, sounding half afraid and half hopeful.

"No, probably not the Wade house," Grandfather said, smiling.

Benny looked relieved. "Look out, ghosts, here we come!"

With Henry reading the directions, Grandfather had no trouble finding Mrs. Wade's house. Like many of the houses they passed, it was a big old house with a wide front porch. Mrs. Wade's house had a porch upstairs and down and was painted white with dark green shutters. An old oak tree draped with moss shaded the front yard. Flower beds bloomed along the front walk and around the house.

"It doesn't look haunted at all," Benny said. "None of the houses we've passed look haunted."

"Maybe that's a ghost!" said Jessie as the front door of the house opened and a small silver-haired woman stepped out. She shaded her eyes with her hands to see the Aldens better.

Grandfather laughed. "That's no ghost. That's Sally Wade."

Mrs. Wade waved at them. "Y'all are just in time for iced tea and cookies," she called. "Come on in."

Benny and Watch ran up the front walk, while the others followed more slowly.

As Benny got closer, Mrs. Wade smiled. Lines crinkled at the corners of her brown eyes. "I think you must be Benny," she said.

"You're right!" Benny cried. "How did you know? Did Grandfather tell you?"

Before Mrs. Wade could answer, he went on, "And this is Watch. And here comes Jessie — she's twelve — and Violet — she's ten. Henry's fourteen, and we don't know how old Watch is, because we found him. I'm not sure how old Grandfather is, either."

"Old enough," said Grandfather, smiling. He came up the steps and gave Mrs. Wade a hug.

"It's so good to see you, James," Mrs. Wade said. "It's been much too long."

Just then, the door opened and two girls of about eighteen or nineteen came out.

"Hi," said Benny. "Did you bring the cookies?"

The taller of the two girls, who wore her dark brown hair pulled back in a ponytail, said calmly, "Not yet. We'll help you bring your luggage in and show you your rooms first. I'm Kate Frances Wade. Mrs. Wade is my grandmother."

She motioned to the girl next to her, who had curly red hair and green eyes. "And this is Elaine Johnston. She's a real practical joker. You have to keep an eye on her!"

"Call me Lainey," the girl said with a warm smile.

"I'm Benny," Benny said. After everyone had been introduced, Kate Frances and Lainey helped the Aldens bring in their suitcases and showed them to their rooms.

Benny especially liked his room, which was across the hall from Henry's. It was small and fitted neatly under the sloping roof at the back of the house. It had a window with a window seat. Benny and Watch knelt on the pillow there and peered out the window. They saw a big backyard with a garden in it.

"It's nice, Watch. But no boxcar," Benny said.

"Boxcar?" asked Kate Frances, who had taken Benny to his room.

"We have a boxcar in our backyard in Greenfield," Benny explained. "We used to live in it when we were orphans."

"You did?" Kate Frances raised her eyebrows in surprise.

"Yes. Before Grandfather found us and we went to live with him," Benny said.

Henry had come into the room and he and Benny told the story of how the Aldens thought the grandfather they didn't know would be mean so they found the old boxcar in the woods and decided to live there.

"That's where we found Watch," Benny put in.

"Then Grandfather found us," Henry explained. "And we went to live with him."

"And he moved the boxcar. It's behind our house in Greenfield now so we can still

visit it whenever we want," Benny concluded.

"That's quite a story," Kate Frances said. "I'm sorry we don't have a boxcar of our own."

"If you had a ghost, it would be almost as good," Benny said hopefully.

"A ghost? Hmmm. Why don't we go have some tea and cookies," suggested Kate Frances.

They went back downstairs and found Grandfather, Jessie, Violet, and Lainey gathered on the porch. Benny spotted the plate of cookies and the pitcher of iced tea on the porch table.

Lainey poured him a glass of iced tea and he took a cookie and went to sit on the porch swing with Jessie.

"I was talking about our jobs at Elbow Bend State Park," Lainey told them. "Kate Frances and I are working there and staying with Mrs. Wade this summer. We just finished our first year at the state university."

Mrs. Wade pushed open the screen door

and came out with a bowl of water, which she put in the corner of the porch in the shade. "For you, Watch," she said.

Mrs. Wade sat down. Kate Frances poured her some iced tea and said, "Benny's been telling me that he wishes we lived in a haunted house."

"Benny!" said Jessie.

"Well, maybe *next door* to a haunted house," said Benny. "I guess I wouldn't want to live with a ghost."

Everyone laughed, and Benny laughed, too.

"I hate to tell you, Sally," Grandfather said, "but I did say that there *might* be a haunted house in an old town like Elbow Bend."

Mrs. Wade's eyes sparkled. "Now, how did you guess?" she said. "We have a town full of ghosts! And even better, Kate Frances is a very good ghost finder!"

CHAPTER 2

# The Ghost Dog of Elbow Bend

"Ghost finder?" Violet's voice squeaked in spite of herself.

"You catch real live ghosts?" Benny asked excitedly.

"But there's no such thing as a ghost. Is there, Grandfather?" Jessie demanded.

"No. Of course not," Grandfather answered.

"I'm not a ghost catcher *or* a ghost finder," Kate Frances said. "I'm a ghost *story* finder."

Henry looked puzzled. "I don't understand," he said.

Kate Frances made a face at her grandmother. Mrs. Wade's eyes crinkled with amusement. "What my grandmother means is that I'm doing research for a special school project on ghost stories. Local ghost stories, to be exact. So I've been interviewing people around Elbow Bend about the ghost stories and tales they grew up hearing."

Lainey said, "After all, just because there is no such thing as a ghost doesn't stop some people from believing the stories, or even thinking they've seen a ghost."

"Are there lots of ghosts in Elbow Bend?" asked Violet, looking around a little nervously.

"They're everywhere," Kate Frances said cheerfully. "It seems like everyone has a story to tell. There's even a famous writer who lives near here who says she has a ghost named Jeffrey living in her house."

"Uh-oh," said Benny.

"But you don't believe in ghosts because

there's no such thing as one, remember, Benny?" Jessie reminded her younger brother.

"Oh, right," said Benny.

"I have an idea," Lainey said. "Now that it's cooling off a little bit, why don't we take a walk?"

The words "take a walk" made Watch raise his head and wag his tail hard.

Lainey went on, "And you can give everyone the ghost-house tour that you gave me when I got here, Kate Frances."

"What a good idea," said Jessie immediately.

Grandfather Alden and Mrs. Wade exchanged glances. "It's still a little hot for me," Grandfather Alden said. "I think I'll stay on the porch a little while longer, and then I'll help Sally start cooking dinner."

"Help is welcome," Mrs. Wade said.

"Okay, then," Henry said. "Let's go!"

Soon the Aldens were walking down the shady streets of the small town. Benny held on to Watch's leash.

Sometimes they would pause and Kate

Frances would tell them stories about the town's houses — and ghosts.

"For example," Kate Frances said, "that house — that's the Pink House." She pointed to a big old house set far back from the sidewalk.

"Is it haunted?" Benny asked.

"Only by the color pink," Lainey told him.

"It's not pink," Jessie objected. "It's just white. With green shutters."

"Ah, but once upon a time, it *was* pink," said Kate Frances, "inside and out. Pink was the owner's favorite color. All the flowers that come up around the house are still pink."

Lainey said, "And they kept one room all pink, too. In honor of the original owner."

Violet rather liked the idea of a house in shades of pink. But since purple was her favorite color, she decided she would prefer a purple house. "Maybe one day I'll live in a purple house," she said aloud.

"With violets all around it," Jessie said.

Violet smiled at the thought.

"Now, there's a house some *do* think is haunted," Kate Frances said as they walked on. This house was smaller, but still big enough to have a wide front porch filled with rocking chairs.

"Is it a good ghost or a bad ghost?" Benny asked.

"A good ghost, I guess," Kate Frances said. "It likes to sit in the rocking chairs on the front porch. People say you can go by on a perfectly still afternoon and one chair will be rocking. Just one."

The Aldens looked at the row of rocking chairs on the front porch. But not one of them moved.

"I guess the ghost isn't out today," Lainey said.

They walked on, up one street and down another. People said hello as they passed and many people knew Kate Frances by name.

"Do you know everybody in Elbow Bend?" Henry asked Kate Frances.

She shook her head. "Not everybody," she said. "But people say hello to everyone

here. They're just friendly, I guess." She smiled and nodded at a woman who was walking by, frowning as she stared at the houses. The woman wore dark glasses, red lipstick, and a big straw hat to protect her from the sun.

"Hello," Kate Frances said.

The woman's dark glasses turned toward Kate Frances. She frowned harder. "Do I know you?" the woman asked.

"No. I was just saying hi," said Kate Frances.

"Oh," said the woman. She turned away and kept walking.

"I guess not *everybody*'s friendly," Henry teased.

Kate Frances laughed. "I guess not," she said.

They paused at a corner while a bus rolled by. People were leaning out the windows of the bus, taking photographs, while a man's voice droned through a loudspeaker inside. Kate Frances nodded toward the bus and added with a mischievous smile, "I don't know all the tourists who come through town."

"How *do* you know so many people?" asked Jessie.

"I've been coming to Elbow Bend every summer since I was a little girl to visit my grandmother, Jessie. That's how I first got interested in ghost stories and folktales, I think. I just loved listening to the grown-ups swap tall tales," Kate Frances said.

"Tall tales?" asked Violet.

"Stories that are just so outrageous they can't be true," said Kate Frances. She stopped. "Now, there's a house with a good tall tale about it."

"Tell it," begged Benny.

"Well, during the full moon in the summer, some say, you can hear the sound of a garden party, right over there behind that wall all covered with jasmine. But if you push open the gate and go inside, the sound stops and nothing is there. Close the gate and come back outside and listen . . . and in a few minutes you'll hear soft laughter and the clinking of glasses."

"Ohhhh," Violet breathed.

"Why? Are they ghosts? Where do they come from?" asked Henry.

"Some people say it's an engagement party for the oldest daughter of the family that lived there long ago. Her fiancé went to war after that and never came back and she died of a broken heart, saying that party was the last happy day she ever had," Kate Frances said, folding her hands over her heart dramatically.

"How sad," said softhearted Violet.

Watch gave a sharp bark.

Lainey looked down and then over at Kate Frances. "Watch says don't forget the ghost dog story."

"Ghost dog? Where does the ghost dog live?" asked Benny.

"Oh, the ghost dog doesn't live anywhere. That's a common ghost story out in the country — here, and in other parts of the world," said Kate Frances. "Sometimes it appears trotting alongside your carriage . . . or these days your car or your bike . . . to warn you of danger.

"The story goes," Kate Frances continued, "that once upon a time, a little dog just showed up in town and made himself at home in the shade of the bench next to the courthouse door. No one knew where he came from or whom he belonged to. He was friendly and several people tried to adopt him, but he wasn't interested. So they fed him and petted him and took care of him as much as he would let them.

"Anyway, he watched the people come and go as if he were waiting for someone, but no one knew who or why. They did know that every once in a while the little dog would stand up and bark — just one sharp bark — at someone who was going into a trial. And when he did, that person was always found guilty. People started calling the little dog 'Judge' and the name stuck.

"Then one day Judge jumped up and started barking like crazy, running around the courthouse and jumping up at the windows. People came running out to see what was wrong, and just about then, the whole building collapsed.

"Well, Judge had saved everyone's life. Somehow, he'd known that building would fall. But when everyone remembered what he'd done and tried to find him to reward him, he was gone. He'd just disappeared. No one ever saw him again. . . .

"Except . . ."

Violet pressed her hands to her cheeks. "Except *when*?" she breathed.

"Except when something terrible is going to happen. Then Judge comes back, waiting and watching and barking and howling to try to warn people. And woe to anyone who doesn't listen to the Ghost Dog of Elbow Bend."

CHAPTER 3

# Howls in the Night

Applause broke out.

The Aldens turned in surprise. They had been so interested in the story that Kate Frances was telling, they hadn't even noticed that a small crowd of people had also stopped to listen. Several of them were tourists, with cameras around their necks.

"That was just wonderful," a large man with a big camera said. "May I take your photograph?"

"Sure," said Benny.

"Me, too, me, too," several other people

said. Cameras clicked. One man even had a video camera trained on them. Kate Frances laughed.

"Wasn't that wonderful, Elizabeth?" a young woman said to the older woman standing next to her. It was the woman in the dark glasses, red lipstick, and big hat.

The woman turned up a corner of her mouth. It *might* have been a smile. "I'm hot," she complained. Then, almost reluctantly, she said to Kate Frances, "That wasn't bad. You could almost be a writer."

"Thanks," said Kate Frances as the group began to wander away.

The younger woman smiled. "Elizabeth should know!" she said brightly.

"Come on. Let's get out of the sun," the woman named Elizabeth muttered.

The group on the sidewalk broke up and people drifted away. Henry looked at his wristwatch. "Wow," he said, "almost time for supper."

"We'd better head back," said Kate Frances.

By the time they got back to Mrs. Wade's

house, the evening shadows of the trees had grown long and the sun was almost down. Grandfather Alden was setting the wooden table inside the screened porch.

Soon dinner was on the table and Watch was eating a bowl of dog food nearby.

"Fried chicken," said Grandfather. "If it tastes as good as it smelled while you were cooking it, Sally, it will be delicious."

"It is," mumbled Benny, who'd already reached for a drumstick and taken a big bite.

While they ate, they talked about everything they'd seen that day.

"When I grow up I'm going to have a purple house just like the pink one," Violet said.

"But it won't be just like the pink one if it is purple," Henry teased her gently.

"When I grow up, I'm going to move to Elbow Bend and eat dinner just like this every day," Benny said.

"Well, we don't eat like this every day, Benny," said Mrs. Wade. "But I'm glad you like my cooking." She looked pleased.

Watch finished his meal and walked to

the edge of the porch. He pressed his nose against the screen. He tilted his head as if he were listening to something that no one else could hear.

"This town has lots of stories in it. But no mysteries so far," Jessie said. "Not real mysteries, anyway."

"You like mystery stories?" Lainey asked.

"Oh, yes," said Jessie. "We like to solve them."

"Solve them?" Lainey looked a bit surprised.

"Sure. We've solved lots of mysteries," Henry said. "Even one with a singing ghost."

Kate Frances laughed. "Well, with all the ghost stories people tell around here, maybe a mystery will turn up yet."

Just then, Watch gave one short, sharp bark, then threw back his head and let out a long howl.

Everyone at the table froze.

Then Benny dropped his fork, pushed back his chair, and hurried over to the small dog. "What's wrong, boy?" he asked.

In answer, Watch howled louder.

"Watch?" said Jessie. "Are you okay?"

Then, as quickly as he had begun, Watch stopped howling. But the fur on his back stayed up and he kept his nose pressed against the screen for a long moment.

Benny wrapped his arms around Watch's neck. Watch turned his head and licked Benny's cheek.

Looking up at everyone at the table, Benny said, "I know what Watch saw. He saw the ghost dog!"

"Benny! You know there is no such thing as a ghost. Or a ghost dog," Jessie said.

Violet didn't say anything. She stared out at the darkness and the fireflies, half expecting to see a ghost dog float by.

"Watch could have been howling at anything," Henry said. "An owl hooting that we couldn't hear. Or a siren far away."

"Come have dessert, Benny," Grandfather said. "I'm sure the reason Watch howled is as simple as a hooting owl. No ghosts."

Benny looked through the screen at the

night, but he didn't see anything. Whatever had caused Watch to howl had stopped — or gone away.

Later that night Benny and Watch came into Henry's room. Benny, who was wearing his pajamas, rubbed his eyes and yawned. Henry looked up from his book.

Benny said, "Watch and I came to say good night."

"Good night," said Henry. "And remember, I'm just across the hall if you get scared or anything."

"Scared?" Benny said. "I'm never scared. Only, maybe, a little worried sometimes."

Henry smiled at his younger brother. "Well, if you get a little worried, just call me. I'll be right here."

"Okay," said Benny. "And if you're worried about the ghost dog, don't be. Watch will protect us."

"There isn't a ghost dog, Benny. That's just a story," Henry said.

Benny looked as if he might want to argue with Henry. But all he said was, "Good night."

"Good night," said Henry.

When Benny stepped into the hall, he saw Lainey, who motioned for him to follow her. "Come on," she said. "We'll help the ghost dog pay Henry a visit."

"How?" asked Benny.

"With an old Halloween mask I found in the closet in my room. It's a basset hound mask."

"You mean, play a joke on him?" ask Benny.

"Yep," said Lainey.

A few minutes later, wearing the dog mask, Benny walked back down the hall. When he reached the door, Lainey turned off the hall light.

No light showed under Henry's door. Benny wondered if his older brother was already asleep.

If he was, Benny and Lainey were about to awaken him!

"Scratch on the door a little, like a dog, but softly," Lainey told Benny.

Benny scratched on a lower panel of

the door. As he did, Lainey let out a soft moan.

Benny thought he heard a sound from Henry's room.

He scratched again. Lainey let out a low howl that sounded pretty scary to Benny.

"What? Who's there?" Henry's voice sounded as if he had been asleep.

Lainey howled once more.

The light in Henry's room came on. He threw open the door. Lainey howled again, and Benny did, too.

Henry jumped back. Then he realized who it was.

"Benny! Lainey!" he exclaimed.

"No, it's the ghost dog," said Lainey, turning on the hall light. She and Benny began to laugh.

Henry shook his head, grinning. "You almost fooled me. Almost."

Benny threw his arms around his brother. "Good night," he said again. "We promise not to let the ghost dog wake you up anymore!"

Henry rolled his eyes. "I'll count on it. Good night."

"That was a pretty good joke," Benny said.

He went into his room and got into bed. Benny put his flashlight by his bed, just in case, then turned out the light and pulled the sheet up to his chin. He stared at the darkness. Was that a ghostly white shape by the window?

He clicked on the flashlight.

No, it was just a vase of white flowers.

Benny yawned. A moment later he was sound asleep.

Violet blinked and sat up in her bed. What had awakened her?

She glanced at the clock by her bed. It was midnight, exactly.

Just as she realized how late it was, Violet heard a low-sounding howl float through her open window. And then another. And another.

*The ghost dog*, Violet thought and grabbed the covers to pull them up around her.

Then another howl, much closer, made her gasp.

It was coming from inside the house!

Violet dropped the covers, grabbed for her robe, and ran out of her room. She just missed crashing into Jessie, who was running out of her room, too.

They heard the howl again.

"Benny's room," Jessie cried. "Hurry!"

Henry bolted out of his room and joined them. He threw open the door of Benny's room and switched on the light.

Benny was kneeling at the window seat, holding Watch's collar. He turned toward them. "The ghost dog!" he cried. "It's here!"

Just then, Watch threw back his head and let out another long howl. It made the hair on Violet's neck stand up, almost like the hair on Watch's neck.

More howls from nearby yards and houses joined Watch's.

And then, just as suddenly as it had begun, the howling died away.

Now the night was perfectly still. Not even the crickets sang.

"Watch, are you okay? What's wrong, boy?" Jessie asked. She went to Watch and patted his head.

Watch didn't seem to notice. He just peered out through the window screen into the night.

"What's going on?" It was Kate Frances, with Lainey behind her. They stood in Benny's doorway.

Benny turned to face everyone. "It was the ghost dog," he said. "It was calling Watch and all the other dogs, too."

"What? That's impossible!" Kate Frances said.

"I *thought* I heard dogs howling," Lainey said.

But Jessie said, "Real dogs, Benny. Only real dogs were howling. In the first place, there's no such thing as a ghost."

"It was probably an animal of some kind he heard," Kate Frances said. "Just like he did during dinner this evening. Maybe a raccoon or a fox is living in the strip of woods along the creek that runs across the bottom of the backyard."

"If it was just an animal, Watch would have barked, not howled," Benny said.

"It's nothing to worry about, Benny," Henry assured him. "Why, Grandfather and Mrs. Wade slept right through it. If it hadn't been for Watch, we probably would have, too."

Benny sighed.

"Let's get some sleep," Henry said. "We've got a big day tomorrow."

Kate Frances was frowning. But she said, "Right. Y'all are going to Elbow Bend State Park with Lainey and me tomorrow."

When everyone had left and the room was dark and quiet again, Benny whispered to Watch, "If you see the ghost dog again, Watch, just howl. And we'll catch it!"

CHAPTER 4

## Clues in the Park

But Watch didn't howl any-more that night and when Benny woke up, sunlight was pouring in through the window. He jumped out of bed and got dressed as quickly as he could.

As he and Watch hurried down the stairs, his nose told him that someone had already made biscuits. He joined everyone else in the kitchen for a breakfast of buttered biscuits with blackberry jam, along with grits and ham. Even Watch got a piece of ham.

Grandfather said to Benny, "I hear Watch

did some midnight singing last night."

"He howled," Benny agreed.

"I understand Watch wasn't the only dog in town who howled at midnight," Mrs. Wade said.

"Something made Watch and all the other dogs howl last night," Benny said.

Jessie shook her head. But she only said, "I think I'm going to have another biscuit."

"Me, too," said Violet. "They are delicious."

"When we're finished with breakfast, it'll be time to go to work," Kate Frances said.

"Are we going to work with you?" Violet asked.

Kate Frances smiled. "Maybe we can find a job for you, if you want one."

Elbow Bend State Park was by a big curve in the river. Kate Frances drove past a small ticket booth and waved at the older man inside, who was wearing an ELBOW BEND STAFF cap. She parked the car in a small parking lot behind a building made of rough-cut wood and led the way inside.

"Good morning, Kate Frances. Good

morning, Lainey." A woman came out of a small office right by the front door.

"Good morning, Ms. Hedge," said Kate Frances. "I've brought some volunteers for the day." She introduced the four Aldens.

"We have plenty of work for you. We need someone to stack all the pamphlets in our information booths and to help hand out maps."

"I can do that," Violet said.

"Me, too," said Benny.

Ms. Hedge said, "Kate Frances, I'm counting on you to help me plan the Stories Under the Stars program. It's only two days away, you know."

"Stories Under the Stars?" asked Henry.

Ms. Hedge nodded. "Yes. There is a storyteller who lives near here. She's a well-known storyteller and she'll be here tomorrow night at our outdoor theater. You should come. She's wonderful."

"We will," said Jessie.

"We can sit in the employee section," Kate Frances said. "My grandmother was already planning on coming and I know your grandfather would enjoy it, too."

"Good," said Ms. Hedge. She turned to Lainey and continued, "The ground crew needs a little help today, Lainey, if you don't mind pitching in. Someone knocked over all the litter containers on Bluff Trail and Overlook Trail."

"Good grief," said Lainey. "Who'd do a thing like that?"

"Maybe it was a wild animal," said Violet. "A raccoon. Or a bear."

"No bears around here," Ms. Hedge said, to Violet's secret relief. "And I doubt a raccoon is strong enough to turn over those big containers." Her lips tightened a little. "No, it was someone's stupid idea of a joke."

"Well, let's get to work," said Lainey. "Henry, Jessie, you want to come along?"

"Sure," said Jessie.

"And we can look for clues," Henry added. "Maybe we can solve the Mystery of the Garbage Can Litterbug."

Lainey laughed. "Maybe. Let's get packs from the equipment room and some sandwiches. We'll have a picnic lunch on the trail."

Kate Frances said, "And we'll have a picnic right here."

"See you this afternoon," Violet said. She and Benny went to work in the visitors' center while Henry and Jessie set out on the trails with Lainey.

"Wow," Jessie said as she stuffed newspaper into the litter sack slung over one shoulder. "Some people sure are litterbugs."

It was hot, hard work. Henry and Jessie looked for clues that might help them figure out who would upend all the litter cans — or why. But there were too many footprints on the trail to point to any one suspect and they could find nothing else that helped.

"Whew! That's done. Let's head back," Lainey said at last. "I just hope whoever pulled the trash can tricks doesn't come back."

"Me, too," said Henry.

As they came out of the woods into the main clearing of the park, Henry said, "What's that old cabin over there?"

"Oh. That's one of the cabins of the original European settlers here," Lainey said. "Or what's left of it. In this corner of the park and back through the woods are what's left of several houses of the people who used to live here over two hundred years ago. Dr. Sage sometimes camps out here. She's the archaeologist in charge of digging up the historic sites in the park. Why don't we go meet her?"

As Lainey, Henry, and Jessie approached the old ruined cabin, a woman peered from around the back of the house. "Stay between the ropes," she barked. "Or you'll be trampling on history."

Henry and Jessie were a little startled by this sharp welcome, but Lainey seemed used to it. "Hi, Dr. Sage," she said. "It's just me. I brought some friends to meet you. This is Henry and Jessie. They're staying with Mrs. Wade and doing some volunteer work in the park."

Dr. Sage came out from around the corner of the house. She was a small, strong-looking woman, with dark skin. Her dark brown eyes seemed to miss nothing. She wiped one hand on the leg of her dirt-smudged jeans and said, "Hello."

Jessie and Henry said hello and shook hands.

"So you're volunteering. That's good. Saves the park money. Money saved is money I can use to do my digging and research," Dr. Sage said.

"I'm glad," Jessie replied politely.

Dr. Sage gave a short laugh. "Just don't mess with anything around our dig. It may look untidy, but we can tell when someone's been here who shouldn't have been. People on the tour groups have actually tried to pick up artifacts to take home!"

Jessie and Henry both were about to protest that they knew better than to touch historic ruins uninvited, but Dr. Sage stopped them by raising her voice and shouting, "Brad! You've got company!"

"Coming," a voice called from the edge

of the nearby trees. A few seconds later a tall, lanky young man with long hair pulled back in a short ponytail came ambling out of the woods. Although it didn't seem possible, he was covered with even more smudges of dirt than Dr. Sage.

"Lainey's here to say hello to you," Dr. Sage said.

"And to introduce some volunteers," Lainey said quickly. Henry noticed that Lainey was blushing. When he looked over at Brad, he thought Brad's cheeks were red, too, but it might have been sunburn.

Brad smiled and shook hands with the Aldens. "Hi, I'm Brad Thompson."

"Are you finding anything interesting?" Henry asked Brad after they'd been introduced.

"As a matter of fact, I've found some very interesting pottery fragments," Brad said. "It leads me to believe that I'm on the right track to the town dump."

"Dump?" ask Jessie, thinking of all the garbage and litter they'd just picked up along the trail.

Brad nodded eagerly. "Yes! Isn't it great news?"

Seeing their puzzled looks, Dr. Sage explained, "If we study what people of earlier times threw away, it can tell us quite a lot."

Jessie laughed. "Wait until we tell Benny that the scientists here are studying *garbage*, especially after we cleaned it up all day."

Lainey shook her head and smiled. "I guess we should go and let you get back to work."

"Good idea," Henry agreed.

They all said good-bye to Dr. Sage and Brad. Brad looked up and said, " 'Bye, Lainey, and, uh . . . everyone."

Dr. Sage didn't even notice that they were leaving.

"Are they always like that?" Henry asked.

"Worse," said Lainey with a little sigh. "Brad and Dr. Sage would work all day and all night if they could. They'd be happy if we closed this park to everyone but scientists and historians."

"But you're practically a historian, aren't you?" Jessie asked.

"I'll be a historian when I finish college. Right now I'm just a history student," Lainey said, with one last glance back at Brad.

"Look," said Jessie. "There's Violet outside the visitors' center."

"And Benny, too," Henry said.

Violet had a map in her hand and was pointing to it while she talked to an attractive woman with sleek black hair. The woman had on tiny square-framed sunglasses and bright red lipstick.

Violet then gave the map to the pretty tourist, who stuffed it into a pocket and walked away.

Benny and Violet hurried over to join Henry, Jessie, and Lainey.

"We've given out about a million maps," Benny said.

No one got a chance to answer because just then an angry voice shouted, "Hey! Stay on the paths, like you're supposed to!"

A tall, strongly built man in work pants, work boots, and a long-sleeved shirt that said ELBOW BEND STAFF stomped up to them. He had a rake in one hand, which he waved. "Can't you read?" he demanded. "What does that sign say?" He gestured toward a small green-and-white sign at the base of a tree.

" 'Please stay on the . . . trails,' " Benny read aloud.

"And where are you standing?" the man growled.

Benny looked down at his feet. He looked over at Violet. "I guess we kind of took a shortcut *between* the trails," he said.

"Huh," said the man. "First you walk right through the leaves I've raked up. Then you go and knock over all my garbage cans. Tourists!"

"We work here," Violet said, finding her voice.

"And we didn't knock over anything," added Benny.

The man stepped back, pushed up his cap, and studied them.

Just then Kate Frances came up the trail. She said, "It's true. These are friends of mine and they're doing some volunteer work."

"Well," the man said grudgingly, "I guess you're not tourists. I guess you're not *so* bad. I'm Joshua Wilson, head of the grounds crew. You can call me Joshua. That's good enough for me."

He paused. "But you still have to obey the rules." He stalked off, waving his rake and muttering to himself.

"Wow. He's grumpy," said Jessie.

"He's proud of this park. It upsets him when people don't treat it right. And you can't blame him for being grumpy after someone knocked over all the garbage containers," Kate Frances told them. "Joshua thinks we should limit the number of tourists allowed in here. He says it would be better for the park."

"Did you find any clues?" Benny asked, turning to Henry and Jessie, just remembering the garbage can mystery.

Henry shook his head.

"Not a single one," Jessie said.

Then Benny remembered another mystery. "Hey, Kate Frances," he said as they walked toward the car to drive home for the evening. "Are there any ghosts in Elbow Bend State Park?"

"Nope," said Kate Frances. "Not even a ghost dog."

But as it turned out, Kate Frances was wrong.

# CHAPTER 5

# *Tourists Keep Out?*

The next morning, as the Aldens walked toward the Elbow Bend State Park visitors' center, they saw Dr. Sage and Brad. Henry and Jessie had told Violet and Benny about the scientist, and Lainey and Kate Frances had promised to introduce them.

But the two girls didn't get a chance.

Dr. Sage turned toward them as they came up, put her hands on her hips, and said, "You children didn't do any volunteer digging last night, did you?"

"No!" said Henry.

"Why? What's wrong?" Lainey asked.

"Someone's been at the site. Whoever it was made several holes. We just reported it," Brad said.

"May we see?" asked Jessie.

"I guess so," Dr. Sage agreed. "Come on."

When everyone reached the site, Dr. Sage led the way on a worn footpath lined by vivid yellow nylon cord strung between metal stakes. Signs taped to the cord said, OFFICIAL STATE HISTORIC SITE and KEEP OFF.

Brad said, "Over here." He stepped over the cord and raised it up so that the others could duck under. Walking carefully around the edge of a shallow rectangle in the earth, Brad pointed.

Next to the rectangle was a deep hole, with dirt flung up messily all around it.

Benny squatted down next to the hole. "Wow," he said. "It looks just like the holes Watch digs. Only bigger."

"It's no dog or wild animal," Dr. Sage

said. "That's not typical behavior for a dog — to go around digging holes all over the place like this."

"And in just one night," said Brad. "Plus, there are no dog or fox footprints. No animal tracks of any kind."

"Did anything get stolen?" Violet asked as they walked from one place to another, examining all the holes.

"No," said Brad. "In fact, I found several pieces of pottery at one of the sites, scattered around with the dirt that had been scooped out."

"Look at this," Benny said as they reached the last hole, on the edge of the site. "It's a *bone!*"

Everyone peered over Benny's shoulder into the bucket-sized hole in the red dirt. Brad leaned down and picked up the small white object.

Brad sniffed the bone. "It's a chicken bone. From a fried chicken dinner, unless I'm mistaken. But what's it doing way out here?"

"I know," said Benny. He looked around

at the others, his eyes wide. "It's the ghost dog! It was burying a bone — but then morning came and scared it away!"

"Ghost dog?" Dr. Sage's features seemed to grow sharper. "Not at my dig!"

"I know that old ghost dog story," Brad said. He smiled. "I don't think it was a ghost dog, Benny. I think someone is playing a stupid joke."

"If I catch who did it, I'll make them sorry they ever thought of doing something like this," growled Dr. Sage. She looked at Brad. "Let's get to work. We'll leave the holes. No use disturbing the site even more."

"We need to get to work, too," Kate Frances agreed.

They all headed back to the visitors' center.

"That's the second time in two days that something weird has happened in the park," noted Henry. "First the garbage getting dumped all over the trails. Then all those holes."

"It does sound a little like something a dog would do, doesn't it?" Jessie said.

"But it's not," Violet said. "It's definitely a person."

"The park is locked at night, or at least the entrance gate is," Kate Frances said. "Whoever did it would have had to sneak in here at night, and there would be . . ."

"Snakes." Lainey shuddered. "They come out at night. I'm afraid of them. We *do* have rattlesnakes around here."

"Not many," said Kate Frances. "And besides, they're more afraid of you than you are of them. They won't hurt you unless you try to hurt them."

"Huh," said Lainey. "I don't want to try to hurt a snake. I don't even want to go *near* one."

They all thought hard for a moment. Then Jessie said, "Maybe someone is mad at the park. Have you fired anyone lately?"

"No," said Kate Frances. "Everyone has worked here for years, except for the summer students, like Lainey and me."

"Maybe it's one of the tourists," said Henry.

"But why?" asked Lainey.

"You could ask Joshua that," suggested Violet. "He thinks tourists are annoying, re-member? He would believe they'd turn over trash cans and dig holes in the middle of the night."

"Yes . . . or maybe Joshua is doing it to make it look like the tourists did it," Henry said.

Lainey looked puzzled. "I don't get it," she said.

"To get the park to limit the number of tourists," Jessie said.

Kate Frances shook her head. "It's an in-teresting idea, but I don't think Joshua would do that. I just can't see him sneaking around in the middle of the night, for one thing."

"Well," said Jessie, "somebody's doing it."

"Or some *ghost*," Benny said under his breath.

"So it looks like we have a mystery to solve after all," Jessie concluded.

* * *

No dogs howled that night. Benny and Watch and everyone else in Mrs. Wade's house slept without being awakened until the sun came up the next morning.

But when they got to the park, they found Ms. Hedge talking to Dr. Sage.

"Dr. Sage looks really unhappy," said Violet softly in Jessie's ear.

Although Violet hadn't meant for Dr. Sage to hear, she did. She turned, folded her arms, and narrowed her eyes at the Aldens. "Dr. Sage *is* unhappy," she stated.

She turned back to Ms. Hedge. "Well. Do we get a night guard? Some kind of security?"

"I'm afraid we can't afford that right now," Ms. Hedge said. "We — "

Dr. Sage snorted. "Figures," she said. Without waiting for Ms. Hedge to reply, Dr. Sage turned and walked away.

The Aldens promptly followed.

"What's wrong?" Henry asked the archaeologist.

"Holes," she said. She was walking so fast

that the Aldens almost had to run to keep up.

"More holes at the site?" asked Jessie, panting a little.

"No. Different holes," Dr. Sage answered.

"What do you mean?" said Benny.

She didn't reply but just kept walking.

And since she didn't object, the Aldens stayed with her. When they reached the site, Dr. Sage led them straight back to where the first hole had been. Brad was squatting by the dig, sifting dirt through what appeared to be a large strainer.

"The detectives are back," said Dr. Sage.

Brad looked up. "Oh," he said. "Uh, did Lainey come with you?"

"Just us," said Benny.

"Well, take a look," said Dr. Sage.

The Aldens went into the roped-off area. The holes from the day before had been filled in, more or less — but other holes had been dug nearby.

"Take a look around," Dr. Sage said. "But watch where you put your feet. Just because someone is dancing around here at night digging holes doesn't mean you can trample over our hard work."

She stalked away.

"Did you find any clues?" Henry asked Brad.

Brad shook his head. "No. Nothing. Not even a chicken bone this time."

The Aldens examined each new hole carefully. All of the original holes had been filled in with dirt. Now there were brand-new holes!

"Why would someone do all this?" Violet wondered.

"Maybe they're looking for something," said Jessie.

Benny saw something in the dirt. He leaned down and gingerly picked up a small scrap of leather. He held it up. It was twisted and covered with dirt. But even so, he knew what it was.

"Look!" he cried. "A dog collar!"

"A dog collar!" exclaimed Violet. "What's a dog collar doing here?"

Brad looked surprised at Benny's find.

"Wow," he said. "If it's real, it'll be a great little piece of history. This is the sort of thing that you put on display for tourists, you know? Perfect for the kind of exhibits they'd pay to see. . . ."

"Is it a really old collar?" asked Henry.

"Hard to say," Brad mused. "Not very much of it left. It's worn. But it's in very good condition for something that would have to have been in the ground for over a hundred years. If it still had any metalwork on it, I could tell right away. They made dog collars by hand back then."

He stood up. "Thanks," he said to Benny, and wandered away toward the small trailer pulled up nearby, where Dr. Sage was reading on the steps.

"I found a clue," Benny said triumphantly.

"You did," agreed Henry. "And maybe two other suspects."

"What do you mean?" Violet asked.

"I know," said Jessie. "You mean that maybe Dr. Sage and Brad dug those holes."

"That's right. To get some publicity. And

maybe to force whoever's in charge to give them some more money for their research," Henry said.

"And I've thought of one more," Jessie said.

"Who?" asked Benny. "Did I find that clue, too?"

"Sorry, no, Benny," Jessie told him. "It's Lainey. I think we have to add her to our list of suspects."

"Lainey!" exclaimed Violet. "Oh, no."

But Henry was nodding. "Because she likes to play jokes, like that joke about the ghost dog she played on me with Benny."

"That's right," agreed Jessie. "Lainey could be doing all of this as a practical joke, a sort of challenge to us as detectives."

Violet said reluctantly, "I guess she could. She *was* awfully interested in the stories about solving mysteries that we told her at dinner our first night here."

"It could even be Lainey *and* Brad," Henry mused. "After all, they seem to like each other."

"They do seem to like each other," said Jessie. "If Lainey thought it would help Brad's work at the dig, she might help him dig holes to get extra publicity."

"Or even to help Dr. Sage!" added Benny.

Holding up her hand, Violet said, "So we have how many suspects? One: Joshua, the head of the grounds crew. Two: Dr. Sage. Three: Lainey. Four: Brad."

"We have a lot more suspects than clues," said Jessie.

"That's happened before," Henry said. "Don't worry. We'll solve this mystery."

"Meanwhile," Jessie said, "let's get to work. And everybody, be sure and keep your eyes and ears open for more clues. You never know when one will turn up!"

Although the Aldens did just what Jessie had suggested, they found no more clues. It was hot outdoors and lots of tourists were visiting the park. As the day was ending, even more began to show up.

"They're here for the storytelling hour,"

Henry said. "It's a good thing we have special reserved seats."

"Grandfather and Mrs. Wade will be here soon, too," said Benny. "I hope they don't forget our picnic dinner."

"They won't, Benny. Don't worry," Violet reassured him.

Just then they passed Joshua Wilson, who was pushing a wheelbarrow toward the tool and gardening shed.

"Good evening, Joshua," said Jessie.

He looked up. Then he looked over at the people following the signs that said, STORIES UNDER THE STARS. He shook his head. "This place will be a mess tomorrow," he said. "Trampled. Full of garbage. Storytelling. Bah!" He pushed the wheelbarrow away to the shed and put it away, still grumbling.

Benny said, "Look. There's Grandfather."

The Aldens hurried to join Grandfather Alden and Mrs. Wade as they made their way toward the outdoor theater. The trail wound through the woods and stopped at a small clearing. In it stood a small wooden stage beneath a curved roof that looked like a large half clamshell. Facing the stage were rows of wooden benches.

Kate Frances waved at them and they made their way to a section of seats near the front. "Here we go," she said. "Just in time for dinner and storytelling."

"Where's Lainey?" asked Henry.

"She's up at the parking lot, directing people," Mrs. Wade answered. "She'll join us if she can."

Henry nodded.

They ate dinner and watched as more and more people arrived. Some had brought picnic dinners, too. As it grew later and darker, soft lights began to shine around the edges of the theater.

Then all the lights went dark for a moment. When they came back on, a hush had fallen over the audience. Spotlighted on the stage was a small woman dressed in a bonnet and old-fashioned clothes.

People applauded and cheered. And then

everyone grew still so that the only sounds were the wind in the trees and the voice of the storyteller.

It had grown late and the storyteller was just finishing when a mournful howl filled the night.

The storyteller stopped. Everyone froze.

Benny grabbed Violet's arm. "The ghost dog!" he cried.

No sooner had he spoken than someone screamed. A man jumped to his feet and pointed. "A ghost. It's a ghost!" he shouted.

# CHAPTER 6

# No Footprints

Some people jumped up to look.

But most of the audience just stared as a small white doglike figure seemed to float through the dark shadows beneath the huge old trees at the far side of the clearing.

And then it was gone.

"Everyone stay calm," said the storyteller. She raised her hands. "I'm glad you enjoyed the conclusion of our performance."

"Oh, it was part of the act," a man near the Aldens said in a relieved voice.

"I knew it wasn't a real dog," said a freckle-faced girl with wiry red hair.

An older woman began to applaud and the rest of the crowd did, too.

Benny, who had jumped up on the bench to see better, turned to Kate Frances. "It was part of the show?" he asked in a disappointed voice.

Kate Frances made a face. "If it was," she said, "no one told me about it."

"So it was real?" Violet gasped.

"I don't know *what* it was," she said. "But as soon as we have seen to it that all the guests have gone, I'm going to find out."

Henry turned to Grandfather Alden. "We need to look into this," he said. "We can get a ride back to Mrs. Wade's house with Kate Frances."

"That'll be fine," said Grandfather, his eyes twinkling.

"Good luck looking for clues," Mrs. Wade added.

"Let's go look for footprints," Jessie said. "A ghost doesn't leave footprints."

They turned to walk to the dark trees at

the edge of the clearing. Henry said, "Violet? Are you coming?"

Violet was looking up at the stage, where Kate Frances was talking to the storyteller. Lainey had joined them, as had several other people. They were all talking and several were holding out pens and paper for an autograph. Violet stared at one of the people in the group who seemed familiar somehow. . . .

"Violet?" Henry said again.

"I remember now!" Violet said suddenly. "I remember where I've seen that woman!"

"Which one?" asked Benny.

"The one with the black hair and the red lipstick. I'm sure it's her," Violet said.

Benny, Jessie, and Henry studied the dark-haired woman. She was talking and waving her hands at the storyteller onstage. Then she held out a book and flipped open the pages.

Jessie said, "Oh. I remember her, too. She was one of the tourists who took Kate Frances's photograph the first day we were here."

"Well, it's too bad she didn't take a picture of the ghost dog," Benny said. He paused, then added, "Of course, you can't really take a picture of a ghost."

"True. But you can look for footprints," said Henry. "Let's go."

But although the Aldens searched all along the edge of the clearing, kneeling on the ground to brush away leaves and covering every inch of ground where the ghost dog had been, they didn't find anything that would help them solve the mystery.

They didn't find a single paw print.

"There *was* a dog," Violet said. "We all saw it!"

"A glowing dog that floated along the ground and didn't leave any footprints," said Henry.

"And we heard it howl," Jessie said. She stopped, frowned, and said, "No, we didn't. The howling happened just *as* the dog was floating by here. But it seemed to be coming from somewhere else."

"Another dog was howling?" asked

Benny. "Well, it wasn't Watch. He's at Mrs. Wade's. If he was howling, we couldn't have heard him."

"Hey! Time to go!" they heard Kate Frances call. She pointed in the direction of the car and then she, Lainey, and the storyteller began to walk up the path.

The Aldens followed. They talked about the case as they walked.

Jessie said, "We've heard dogs howling in town. And now we saw a ghost dog here and heard a dog howling," she went on.

"And someone, or something, is digging holes where Dr. Sage and Brad are working," Violet said.

"Someone has also tipped over garbage cans along trails," Jessie said. "So it looks as if someone is working against the Elbow Bend State Park."

"What's that got to do with a ghost dog howling in town at midnight?" Benny asked.

"Maybe nothing. Maybe that isn't part of the mystery, Benny. Maybe it's just a coincidence," Violet said. "And maybe there's no ghost dog in the town of Elbow Bend. After all, we haven't seen one there."

Ahead of them, the others reached the parking lot.

"Look, there's Joshua," said Henry.

They watched as the grounds-crew chief picked up a piece of paper and put it into a nearby trash can, with a glare at the remaining people. He opened the passenger door of a station wagon and they saw another groundskeeper driving. "Thanks for the ride," they heard Joshua say. "I don't know when that car of mine will be fixed."

Joshua slammed the door and the car drove away. Then the storyteller got into her car and drove away, too. Now only Lainey and Kate Frances and a few of the audience members were left.

"There *is* a ghost dog in Elbow Bend," Benny insisted. "Even if we haven't seen it, we've heard it!"

They'd reached the parking lot now, and everyone heard Benny's words. Faces turned in their direction.

"Ghost dog in Elbow Bend?" the woman with the dark hair cried. "Did you say you'd seen it there?"

"No. I've just heard it. I only saw it tonight," Benny said.

Some people stopped walking and turned to listen. The woman turned to Kate Frances and Lainey and said in a loud voice, "See? I knew it wasn't part of the show. I knew the ghost dog was real! And you owe it to the public to tell the truth about what's going on in this town, as well as everything that's happened in this park!"

The woman looked from Kate Frances to Lainey. Kate Frances just shook her head. "There is no such thing as a ghost," she said. "There's a logical explanation for all of this, and we don't need to frighten people with old ghost stories."

"You have to tell people the truth," said the woman, and marched away across the parking lot and down the road.

Kate Frances said, "Great. Why is this happening all of a sudden? I think she's some kind of writer. Probably a reporter.

This'll probably turn up in the news."

Brad, who was standing by Lainey, said, "Too bad Dr. Sage was at that dinner party. She'd have been very interested in all of this."

"Well, don't worry," Lainey said to Kate Frances. "We'll just pretend none of this happened."

"Yes," said Kate Frances. "But somehow, I don't think ignoring it is going to make our troubles go away."

"OOOOooooohhhh! OOOOooooohhhh!" Loud howls sounded in the night.

Benny sat up. He grabbed for the lamp on the bedside table and flicked the switch. Light flooded his bedroom as Watch answered the ghostly noise with a howl of his own.

The door opened and Henry came in. "Are you okay, Benny?"

Before Benny could answer, more howls rose up from all around the neighborhood. Dogs all over Elbow Bend were joining in the ghostly chorus.

"Twelve midnight exactly," Jessie said, coming in behind Henry, with Violet on her heels.

Suddenly Watch flattened his ears and barked.

Benny ran to the screen and tried to see out.

"Turn out the light," Henry said. "We can see out better without it."

Violet switched off the light.

Almost at once Watch barked again, a short warning bark. At the same time, Benny cried, "There it is! The ghost dog!"

The Aldens crowded around the window. Sure enough, at the foot of the lawn, a small white figure was floating along the ground, rising and falling.

"Come on! We can catch that dog!" Jessie said. She turned and ran out of the room.

"Get your flashlight, Benny," Henry said. "Let's go."

The Aldens thundered down the stairs of the old house, through the hall, and out the kitchen door into the backyard.

Behind them, they heard Grandfather call, "What's wrong?"

"The ghost dog!" Benny called over his shoulder.

With their flashlights crisscrossing the night, they ran across the long sloping lawn.

The dog was nowhere to be seen.

Watch barked again and raced into the woods.

"Watch! Wait for us!" Benny called. He ran after the small, brave dog, wondering what he would do if he and Watch actually caught the ghost.

They thrashed through the trees, ran through the backyard of another house, and came out on a street. Watch stood under a dim streetlight, staring up the road. He was growling in a soft disapproving way when the Aldens reached him.

"Did you see the ghost?" Benny asked. He dropped to his knees and hugged Watch. "Good dog!"

Violet said, "Why would a ghost run out to a street and then disappear?"

"I have a better question," said Jessie.

"How could Watch smell a ghost to track it this far? Only a *real* dog would have a smell!"

"The howling has stopped," Violet said. "Listen."

It was true. Now the night sounds of crickets and the wind in the trees were all they could hear.

"I guess we'd better get back," Henry said. "But this time, we'll use the street instead of cutting through someone's backyard!"

As they walked back, Jessie said, "It's definite. The ghost dog is part of the mystery at Elbow Bend State Park."

"Trash cans tipped over, holes dug, dogs howling, and a glowing white dog that doesn't leave footprints." Violet reeled off the list of events.

"It doesn't make sense," Henry said. "Why would the dog appear at the park, and here, in town, in our backyard?"

They'd almost reached the house when Jessie stopped. "Let's go take another look in the woods," she said. "I have an idea. But first . . ." Untying her bathrobe, she took the sash and looped it through Watch's collar.

"What're you doing that for?" asked Violet.

"You'll see," said Jessie mysteriously.

Once more, but at a slower pace, Jessie led the way across Mrs. Wade's big backyard on the trail of the ghost dog. "Here, Watch," she said when they'd reached the trees at the foot of the yard. "Find the dog. Find the dog."

Watch immediately began to tug on the sash. He pulled Jessie along through the woods, his nose to the ground. He zigzagged in and out among trees and through bushes.

Suddenly Jessie hauled back on the makeshift leash. "Whoa, Watch," she said. Turning her flashlight slightly to one side of where Watch stood expectantly, she said, "There. See it?"

"It . . . glows," Violet said.

"What is it?" Benny asked.

Henry bent over the dash of white on the

rough trunk of a tree. He touched it and pulled back a finger. "It's wet," he said.

"It's paint," said Jessie.

"Glow-in-the-dark paint!" Violet explained.

"That's why we saw a dog that glowed in the dark," Jessie said. "Someone had put paint on part of its coat."

"It's not a ghost?" Benny asked.

"Not at all. This is proof," Henry answered, holding up his paint-dotted fingertip.

"But how could whoever did this make the dog float?" Violet asked. "And why? And why dig the holes and turn over the trash cans? Why would they want everyone to believe that a ghost dog is haunting Elbow Bend?"

"I don't know," said Henry.

The Aldens began to walk back toward the house.

"It could be Joshua, trying to scare tourists away from Elbow Bend," said Jessie. "He was at the storytelling session, but we didn't see him when the ghost dog appeared. And it would be easy for him to sneak into the park and turn over trash cans and dig holes."

"Yes. He's a very good suspect. But it does seem as if the appearance of a ghost dog would bring more tourists, rather than fewer," mused Henry.

"Maybe." Jessie thought for a moment. "And don't forget Joshua's car is broken. He couldn't drive here in the middle of the night without a car that worked."

"Unless someone was helping him," said Violet.

"Maybe . . . but what about Lainey? She could be playing a practical joke."

"Yes. We didn't see her tonight at all, until after the ghost dog had come and gone," agreed Violet reluctantly. She didn't want it to be Lainey. She liked her.

"Or Dr. Sage, to raise money for the park and her digging project," Henry said. "She wasn't even at the storytelling session. But maybe she didn't come so she could sneak up and make us believe we'd seen — and heard — a ghost dog."

"Don't forget Brad," Benny said. "He was there, too."

"Yes. But again, we didn't see him until after the ghost dog had appeared and then disappeared," Violet said. "He could be helping Dr. Sage — or Lainey."

"We have lots of suspects," Benny said. "How do we pick out the person who did it?"

"That's the mystery, Benny," said Henry. "And I'm not sure how we're going to solve it."

# CHAPTER 7

# An Exciting Discovery

"I don't have to work at the park this morning, so I'm going to walk to town to do a little shopping," Lainey said the next morning after breakfast. "Who wants to come with me?"

"I do," said Benny.

"Me, too," echoed Jessie and Violet.

"Count me in," Henry said.

"And I've got to get to work," said Kate Frances. "See you later."

Benny put Watch's leash on and the Aldens and Lainey began to walk to town.

As always, everyone they passed said hello. And as usual, it was very hot. They walked slowly, and Watch panted a lot.

When they got to Main Street, Lainey said, "If you want to look around while I shop, why don't we meet again in an hour? We can meet in the bookstore."

"Okay," said Henry.

After Lainey had left, Violet said, "Let's just walk around and look in all the shop windows."

The Aldens soon discovered that the town of Elbow Bend wasn't so different from their hometown of Greenfield. Like Greenfield, it had a hardware store, an antiques store, a bike shop, a shoe-repair shop, a pet-supply store, an ice-cream parlor, and a gift shop.

"Wow," said Benny, "look at all those cameras!"

They watched as the tourists wandered in and out of the souvenir and T-shirt shops and took photographs of one another.

The Aldens decided to walk into the pet store.

"What a cute dog," said the girl in the store.

"He's hot and thirsty," said Benny.

"Could you let us have a bowl of water for him, please?" asked Violet.

"Sure," said the girl. "I'll go get one right now."

She soon returned with a red bowl filled with water and set it down for Watch. He drank noisily. The Aldens looked around the store.

"You have a nice store," Jessie said.

"Thank you," the girl said. She grinned. "It's not my store, it's my brother's. I just work here so I can get free supplies for Squeeze."

"Squeeze? Who is Squeeze?" asked Henry.

The girl grinned even more broadly and pointed.

The Aldens turned. A large snake was coiled around the branch of a small tree growing out of an enormous pot in the window.

Benny took a step back. "Uh-oh," he said.

The girl said, "Don't worry. Squeeze won't hurt you. He's a boa constrictor and not poisonous. Isn't he beautiful?"

Looking at the snake made Violet nervous, so she looked somewhere else. "Oh," she said. "Look, Watch. Sweaters for dogs!"

"Not that dogs need sweaters very often in this part of the country," the girl commented. "Too hot. They don't usually need those little booties, either. Those are for dogs that live in places with snow, where they put salt on the sidewalk. The salt hurts the dogs' feet. I did sell a set of those booties a few days ago. A whole crowd of people came in the store at once, buying all kinds of things. Some tourists will buy anything!"

Glad to be out of the heat, the Aldens began to look around the store. Benny and Watch took a closer look at Squeeze, being careful not to get *too* close. Henry and Violet bent to study the tropical fish in the big aquarium next to the counter.

Jessie let her eyes wander across the pegboard hung with dog supplies: booties and sweaters, raincoats and fancy collars, in every imaginable color; bones and treats; whistles and toys. . . .

She reached out and picked up a small, thin, silver whistle. She held it up. "About this whistle — " she began.

"Look, there's Lainey!" Benny said. He waved, then dashed to the door and opened it. "Hey, Lainey. We're in here!"

Lainey followed Benny inside the store — and began to scream.

"Nooo!" she shrieked, jumping back and dancing from one foot to the other as if her shoes were on fire. "Eeeek. Oooh! A snaaaaaaake!"

Henry raced over and grabbed Lainey's arm. "This way," he said, and led her outside.

"We'll be right back," Jessie promised. The Aldens all went outside to join Henry and Lainey.

Lainey was pale, with splotches of red on her cheeks. "Sorry," she said. "The snake caught me by surprise. If I'd known it was there, I would never have gone in."

"You *are* afraid of snakes, aren't you?" asked Jessie.

"Terrified," Lainey admitted. "I try not to be, but I can't help it. . . ." Her voice trailed off and she shook her head.

"That's very brave of you to work at the park, then," Violet said, trying to make Lainey feel better.

Lainey managed to smile. "Not so brave. I stick close to the trails and places where I know the snakes aren't likely to be. And I wear big hiking boots that come up almost to my knees. When I had to help out during Stories Under the Stars, I worked in the parking lot directing cars. I didn't even come down to the storytelling until Brad came along to walk with me. That's how afraid I was."

The Aldens exchanged glances. Lainey's confession had just eliminated two of their suspects. There was no way Lainey could have had anything to do with the ghostly dog flitting through the woods around the edges of the storytelling crowd.

"Well, you're safe now," said Henry.

"But if you don't mind," Jessie said, "we'd like to go back into the pet-supply store for a minute."

"Why?" asked Benny.

"You'll see," Jessie said.

Lainey said, "Go on. I'll be at the bookstore. See you in a little while."

"Let's go," said Jessie. The Aldens went back into the store and Jessie went straight to the whistle she'd been holding. "I'd like to buy this," she said.

"The silent whistle? Sure," said the girl. She took Jessie's money and counted out the change.

As Jessie slipped the whistle into her pocket, she said casually, "Have you sold any of these lately?"

"Sure," said the girl.

"To the same person who bought the booties?" Jessie asked.

The girl frowned. "I don't know about that. The store was jammed. I just remember selling the booties because it was so unusual, you know? I *think* it was a lady. But what she looked like, I couldn't tell you. I

remember the booties were white, though. Silly color. Shows dirt."

"Hmmm," said Jessie.

"Thanks for all your help," Violet said. "We really appreciate it."

Jessie nodded. "I think you just helped us solve a mystery."

CHAPTER 8

# Setting a Trap

Benny's eyes grew wide. "What?" he gasped.

Jessie didn't answer right away. They went outside and Benny hopped excitedly along next to her.

"We know Lainey's not the one who did it, because she really *is* afraid of snakes, and we know Brad was with her the other night when everyone saw the ghost dog at the storytelling," Henry said. "Is that what you mean?"

"Nope," Jessie said. She held up the

whistle in its package. "This is what I mean. This is a very important clue."

Violet leaned forward and read aloud from the package, " 'Silent dog whistle. You can't hear it, but dogs can. From as far away as a quarter mile or more.' "

"Silent whistle?" Benny asked. "How can a whistle not make any sound?"

"It does make a sound. It's just such a high-pitched sound that only dogs can hear it," Henry said. He was beginning to figure out the mystery, too.

They'd begun to walk back along Main Street.

"Can I try it? Can I blow the whistle?" Benny asked.

"May I," Jessie corrected him automatically, just as Grandfather would have. "Okay, Benny, give it a try."

Benny pulled the whistle from the cardboard and held it to his lips. He blew hard.

No sound came out. But Watch jumped up at Benny, his ears straight up.

Benny blew again. Again no sound came out.

Watch gave a short sharp bark. Across the street, a black Labrador retriever veered sharply and began pulling on his leash as if he wanted to run toward Benny.

"That's enough, Benny," said Jessie.

Violet said, "Wow, it works. It really works. And if you blew the whistle enough, I bet every dog that heard it would start howling and trying to find out who was whistling."

"But who would do it?" Violet asked. "And why?"

"I think whoever did it was the same person who bought the booties. The ground was not damp enough to show any footprints — especially with that person's dog wearing the booties. The dog turned into a ghost!" Jessie told them.

"The girl at the store said she was pretty sure a woman had bought the booties," Violet said. "That means it wasn't Joshua."

"That just leaves Dr. Sage," Henry said.

"I like Dr. Sage," Benny said. "I don't think she's bad."

"But she does have a good reason — she

wants more money for her work. A ghost dog means publicity, and publicity might help her get more money for research," Henry said.

"Who else could it be?" Jessie said.

"Wouldn't the girl in the store know Dr. Sage?" Violet asked.

"Not necessarily. Dr. Sage isn't from around here. And if she went into the store when a bunch of tourists were in there, the girl might not notice her," Jessie argued.

But they didn't get to suspect Dr. Sage much longer. They ran into her coming out of the hardware store.

"Hi, Dr. Sage," said Jessie.

"Found the hole-digger yet?" was her answer.

"Not yet," said Henry. Was this all a clever game Dr. Sage was playing so they wouldn't be suspicious?

"Did you have a nice time at your dinner party?" asked Violet.

"Dinner parties," said Dr. Sage scornfully. "I sat there from eight o'clock until midnight with the mayor and a state senator.

I'd better get some more money for my project, it was so boring!" With that, she stomped away.

Jessie raised her eyebrows. "I guess Dr. Sage really was at the dinner party," she said.

"And that means she couldn't have done it," said Benny.

"We're completely out of suspects," said Henry.

They walked slowly on, not speaking again until they reached the bookstore. Lainey was waiting for them by the front door. "Ready to go home for lunch?" she asked.

"Yes!" said Benny, to no one's surprise.

They began to walk back through town, but Violet stopped and stared at the bookstore window. "Look," she said. "There she is!"

"There who is?" Henry asked.

"The lady who took Kate Frances's picture that first day," Violet said. "The same one who was saying she was going to tell everyone about the ghost dog at Stories Under the Stars the other night. That's her picture on the poster in the corner of the window."

"You're right," Jessie said.

" 'Book signing,' " Henry read from the poster. " 'By Elizabeth Prattle, author of *The Lady and the Midnight Ghost.*' She's here signing books tonight at the bookstore."

"Listen to this." Henry read aloud again, " 'The story of a lady haunted by a special kind of ghost in an old house in the historic town of Ankle Bend.' "

"Ankle Bend?" Violet giggled. "Just like Elbow Bend!"

"It probably *is* Elbow Bend," Lainey said. "She probably just changed the name a little, in case anyone thought they recognized themselves in there."

"Wow," said Violet. "A famous author."

"Not so famous. I think this is her first book, and it's not on any best-seller lists yet that I know about," Lainey said as they began to walk home.

"I guess she knows a lot about ghosts," said Benny. "Maybe that's why she was so upset about the ghost dog."

"That's it! That's it! I have it!" Jessie cried. "Benny! You just solved another mystery!"

"I did?" Benny asked.

Henry looked at Jessie. He said, "I think I know what you're thinking. But we need to prove it . . . and I think I know how!"

"How? Who did it?" Benny almost shouted.

"Here's the plan," said Henry. He looked at Lainey. "And we'll need you and Kate Frances to help us."

"Wow. There sure are a lot of people here," Benny said. It was after dinner, and the Aldens had returned to the bookstore to set their plan in action.

The lady standing next to him said, "Oh, it's because of the ghost! Haven't you heard about it?"

"Sort of," Henry said quickly, in case Benny gave anything away.

"Isn't it amazing? A ghost! Just like in the book!" the woman gushed, clutching her copy of *The Lady and the Midnight Ghost* to her chest.

"There's a ghost dog in the book?" asked Violet.

"Well, no. Actually, it's a horse. But it's almost the same," the woman said. She moved away.

Jessie rolled her eyes.

"Look," Henry said. "Lainey and Kate Frances are talking to her now."

The Aldens edged closer, so they could hear but not be seen by Elizabeth Prattle.

"So we were wondering if you'd like to do a reading, as part of our Stories Under the Stars program. Could you do it tomorrow night? I know it's not much notice, but — "

"Oh, I think I could manage that," Ms. Prattle interrupted. She smiled and signed another book, then turned back to Kate Frances.

"Wonderful," said Kate Frances. "About seven-thirty? You can read and maybe answer questions, and after we take a break you can read some more and then sign books. How does that sound?"

"Fine," said Ms. Prattle. "I'll be there."

"Great," said Kate Frances. "We'll start letting everybody know."

Lainey said, as if it had just occurred to her, "Wow. What if the ghost dog shows up again? Wouldn't that be amazing? I bet people will come just to see if — "

"Lainey, there is *no* ghost dog," Kate Frances said sternly. "Come on, let's get to work."

Ms. Prattle watched them go with a little smile on her lips, and the Aldens watched Ms. Prattle.

CHAPTER 9

# Whose Ghost Dog?

"The crowd is just as big for Ms. Prattle as it was for the other story-teller," said Kate Frances. "And nobody even knows her around here." She shook her head before hurrying away to help.

"It's because of the ghost stories. The ghost dog," said Henry.

It was true. As the visitors streamed past them to claim seats in the clearing, they heard snatches of conversation. Almost everyone was talking about the ghost dog.

Then Kate Frances walked onto the stage

to introduce Elizabeth Prattle. The audience fell silent, then cheered as the author walked onstage. She stepped up to the podium, took a sip of water, and smiled. "Welcome to all you believers in good writing — and in ghosts!" she said.

With lots of exaggeration and hand gestures, Ms. Prattle began to read.

No one in the audience seemed to mind the exaggeration. They applauded loudly when Ms. Prattle finished reading, and asked her lots of questions. She talked about how her research had led her to believe that many of the ghost stories she'd heard could be true.

Then it was time for a half-hour break.

Henry slipped his flashlight out of his pocket. "Come on," he said to Violet. "Let's go." He and Violet hurried up the trail toward the parking lot.

People wandered toward the concession stand. Kate Frances and Ms. Prattle walked up the stone steps that divided the two rows of benches where the audience sat to listen. Ms. Prattle stopped and spoke to several people and smiled. But she didn't sign any books. "Not until after it's over," she said. "And don't forget, more books will be for sale!"

The Aldens passed Kate Frances. They knew she was offering to walk with Ms. Prattle. "No, no," said Ms. Prattle. "I need a little time to myself. I'll just walk along the trail and think. Don't worry. I'll be back in time to read again!"

She took a flashlight out of her shoulder bag and moved away up the trail.

Jessie and Benny stayed where they were, watching and waiting.

Nothing happened. A few people drifted back to their seats. Benny whispered, "Where's the ghost dog?"

"I don't know, Benny," said Jessie.

Just then, someone screamed.

"It's the ghost!" a woman shouted.

"The ghost dog!" another voice added.

Even though they'd been expecting it, Benny and Jessie both jumped.

Then they saw it: a white figure moving in and out among the trees.

"Come on!" Jessie said.

She and Benny ran toward the dog, skirting the crowd of people who were trying to back away from it. They dashed to the edge of the woods as the dog disappeared into it.

Jessie pulled the silent whistle from her pocket and raised it to her lips. She blew a blast on it. And then another. And then again.

Benny held his breath.

And then the ghost dog reappeared!

It ran toward them. Then it stopped and turned its head as if listening to something only it could hear. It turned.

Jessie blew harder and harder on the whistle. The dog ran forward, then back, then forward.

Benny ran toward the dog. "Here, dog," he called. "Nice ghost dog!" He pulled a dog biscuit from his pocket and held it out.

The dog stopped at the edge of the shadows. It looked utterly confused. As Benny ran up to it, he saw that it wasn't a ghost dog after all — just a white dog covered with something to make it glow, and wearing booties on its feet.

Pulling a collar with a leash attached to it from his other pocket, Benny slipped the collar over the dog's head. "Good dog," he said. "Good girl."

The dog whined a little and looked anxiously over her shoulder. Then she took the biscuit from Benny's hand and allowed herself to be led out into the light.

"It's a dog!" someone said.

"It's not a ghost at all," said someone else.

Jessie bent to pat the dog.

Just then, Ms. Prattle appeared at the top of the stone steps. The dog saw her and strained on the leash, barking and wagging her tail.

Ms. Prattle walked toward the stage as if she didn't see the dog.

And she really didn't see Henry and Violet following her.

She walked up onto the stage and turned to face the audience. She opened her book, although almost no one was sitting down. Faces turned toward her.

"In this chapter — " Ms. Prattle began.

But she didn't get to continue. Benny let the dog drag him up to the stage. Wagging her tail even harder, the dog jumped up and barked happily at Ms. Prattle.

Ms. Prattle looked down.

Jessie stepped forward. "She's your dog, isn't she?" Jessie asked in a loud clear voice.

"I don't know what you're talking about!" Ms. Prattle said.

Henry said, "We followed you to your car just now, Ms. Prattle. We saw you take your dog out. We saw the whole thing."

Slowly Ms. Prattle closed her book. She nodded. Then she knelt down and held out her arms. "Come here, girl. Come here, Dusty. Good girl," she said. And the dog ran into her arms.

Kate Frances said, "Show's over! Everybody go home."

CHAPTER 10

## *The Ghost Catchers Explain*

The porch swing creaked as Benny and Violet rocked back and forth in it. Curled in the corner, Watch yawned.

It was late, long past dinner, on the last night of the Aldens' visit to Elbow Bend. Mrs. Wade had made another special dinner, almost as good as the first one, with peach cobbler and ice cream for dessert.

Now they were all sitting on the porch, talking about the visit — and about solving the mystery.

"I almost forgot to tell you the good

news," Kate Frances said. "More funding is being given to Dr. Sage's research project."

"Isn't that great?" Lainey added. "That means she can pay Brad to keep working for her and maybe even get a second assistant."

"And I think one of the reasons she got the money was because of all the publicity about the fake ghost dog," said Brad. He'd joined them for dinner and was sitting next to Lainey on the wicker sofa.

"I still can't believe that writer, Elizabeth Prattle, would do all that," said Mrs. Wade. She shook her head. "Some people!"

"She got the idea when she overheard Kate Frances telling ghost stories. That was our first day in Elbow Bend and Kate Frances was giving us a tour of the town," Violet said. "She heard the ghost dog story then, saw how the other tourists reacted. She realized it might be useful to her to help sell her book — since her book is based on the same story."

"And she had her dog with her. Dusty. And Dusty was already trained to come to the silent whistle," Henry added.

"That first night, she just used the whistle as an experiment," Benny said. "That's what made all the dogs bark and howl — except her dog, who's used to the whistle."

"And then she went to Elbow Bend State early in the morning and turned over trash cans and dug holes and planted that dog collar to make it look like a dog had been through there," Violet said.

"And then at Stories Under the Stars, she parked her car away from all the others so no one would see her dog inside," Jessie began.

"But wait," Brad said. "How did she make it glow? And leave no footprints?"

"The glow came from glow-in-the-dark Halloween paint," Violet said. "She washed it off Dusty each time. And she put booties on her dog to keep her from leaving footprints."

"Everybody believed Dusty was a ghost," Jessie said.

"She made the howling by playing a tape recording of a dog howling," added Violet.

"And then, after listening to us talk about

the ghost dog in the parking lot, she decided to make the ghost dog appear in town. So she took her dog to the woods along the back of this house and did the same thing," Jessie said.

"Only this time, Watch tracked Dusty, and we found a spot of wet phosphorescent paint on a tree trunk where Dusty had brushed against it," Henry said. "That's when we knew we weren't chasing a ghost but a real dog."

"But how did you know who did it?" Lainey asked.

Violet blushed a little in the dark, and was glad Lainey couldn't see her.

Jessie said, "We had a few suspects. But we were able to narrow the list down and set a trap."

"And we caught her!" Benny concluded triumphantly.

"You sure did, Benny," said Grandfather.

"She got a lot of publicity," said Kate Frances. "But I don't think it was the kind she wanted."

"Her book is still selling well at the bookstore," said Mrs. Wade. "But I think she's sorry she did what she did."

"She sure left town in a hurry," Kate Frances said. "I don't think she'll try anything like that again."

"Well, it's sure been an exciting visit," Mrs. Wade said. "I hope y'all come again soon."

"We will," said Benny. "And we'll catch more ghosts next time!"

"Oh, Benny," Violet said, and everyone laughed.